# WHISPERED CURSES

HALEY TRAVIS

# PROLOGUE
## EDEN


** Nana's Whispers **

We'd always called it The Knowing. It sounded quite mysterious. Well, it was. Nobody in my family was particularly superstitious. I mean, not walking under ladders isn't to avoid bad luck, that's a basic safety tip. And nobody wants to break a mirror – you'd be pulling bits of glass out of the carpet for years.

Yet there was something different when Nana made a proclamation. We would be in the middle of a regular conversation, gathered around the kitchen table. She'd be sipping some strange tea that she had mail-ordered directly from the factory. Apparently, Canadian teas didn't understand true balance, or some complicated British fussiness.

Nana would stare into her teacup, swirling it gently. Her head would cock slightly forward, and to the left. Then she would stare up at the ceiling as the room got quiet. We knew that whatever she was about to say next would be important, and someone would grab the grocery list notepad from the fridge to jot it down.

When Mom was looking for a smaller house after Dad died five years ago, Nana had interrupted our discussion of the importance of a flower garden. Staring up at the ceiling, she had whispered, "Your neighborhood is your garden. Live well, and make it grow."

Mom had been looking in the Junction, and the distant edges of Parkdale trying to find an affordable house. But with this new direction, she found the perfect little bungalow in Woodbine Gardens. It had been underpriced because the decor was so violently hideous. Two weeks of ripping out seventies wallpaper and painting everything in light, soft tones made the house absolutely perfect. The woodwork was still crazily outdated, but Mom liked it.

A few years later, my sister Eva was telling us all about some fancy arts event that her friend was throwing the next Saturday night. She was volunteering to work the door. She was rather excited that she got to dress up like a princess, and welcome people to the ballroom. It sounded adorably kitschy.

Then we all held our breath when we noticed Nana was staring into her teacup. When she glanced up at the ceiling, she whispered, "Rain is plain and snow will blow, but never drive in the freezing rain."

Sure enough, when Eva was coming back from the party at two in the morning after helping to clean up the event, there was half an hour of freezing rain. Instead of waiting for it to pass, she jumped into a taxi.

The accident wasn't too bad, relatively speaking, and she walked away with slight whiplash and a broken wrist. Still, had she heeded Nana's whispers, and just waited half an hour, that wouldn't have happened.

Although Nana had never said anything directly to me, I knew that it would be coming someday. Sometimes her warnings were a bit abstract, such as, "A little of this bologna. No, no no, that's wrong."

Two days later the news was filled with product recalls from a packaged sandwich meat company. Coincidence? We didn't know. Even though we didn't quite believe that she had some sort of gift, or second sight, we all silently agreed that it was better to just do as Nana said.

About six months ago, when I was reeling from a recent devastating breakup, I went to have tea with Nana. She lived in Vancouver now, but was visiting my mother in Toronto for a few weeks.

Nana shared the stories of her love life before she met grandpa. Stories of her lousy, screaming drunk of a first husband. Back in the fifties, women didn't often pick up their baby and move away from their husband. Nana always had a mind of her own.

"How did you know he wasn't going to come after you?" I had asked.

She rolled her eyes at me, sipping her tea. Then she shrugged. "He was always wildly drunk, and he drove a motorcycle. I knew it was just a matter of time."

Sure enough, her first husband wrapped himself around a tree, and Nana met a dashing young military man a year later at a legion hall dance.

They had moved to Canada and started a wonderful new life together. Somehow, hearing the tale of her life again had grounded me. There was always hope. There was always a way to find love.

I was actually smiling to myself when I realized that Nana had grown quiet. She stared down at her tea, swirling it gently as her head fell to the side. Then she stared up at the ceiling.

I could barely make out her whisper, "Never get in bed with the devil. He lives for darkness and fire."

# 1

---

EDEN



They say time heals all wounds. That's not always true.

But tequila helps. A lot.

There is some mathematical formula about how many months it takes a broken heart to heal, according to how many months you were together. It likely didn't take into account if it was your first crack at love, and how you broke up.

Or the fact that there were distinct rumors he had a sugar baby, or some sort of floozy on the side. Not the sort of thing anyone wants to find out the week after a lousy breakup. Perhaps it was the cherry on top of the messed up sundae I'd be telling a therapist about years down the road.

I wasn't ready for many things yet. Bars, drinking, loud people, and Kelly dragging me onto the dance floor after a few shots of tequila. I knew it had been six months, but I didn't know if I'd ever be ready to look at guys again.

We'd gotten ready at Kelly's place, and she practically

forced me to wear one of her saucy party dresses. "Show off those amazing legs," she laughed, fluffing my hair. "Let some men check you out."

"You know I'm not ready for this," I grumbled. But I couldn't resist doing a twirl in front of the mirror. This bright cherry red really did look incredible on me, making my hair look more auburn than brown.

"You don't have to talk to any of them," Kelly laughed, hustling me downstairs and into a cab. "Just ogle them. They're nothing but eye candy tonight."

Sometimes it was great having a friend who took charge, even when she was pushy. Kelly's forthright attitude was encouraging, and usually what I needed.

My perpetually effervescent best friend might have had a point. Men stare at women all the time, with no intention except to admire them and have a little thrill. Was there any reason why I didn't deserve a mental boost?

Her pushiness continued when we arrived at the club, slipping bills to the doorman so that we could skip the line and head straight to the bar. Before I had a chance to think, there were two tequila shots in front of me. Kelly knew my favorite dancing drink well.

"As your party director tonight, I demand that you chug those, then stare at men."

I'd always been the shy one. The girl with her nose in books, where the people were quiet and dependable. The girl who thought things through for days before considering making a move. The girl who wanted things to be planned, and expected. Just this once, I was going to obey, and go with the flow. The worst thing that could happen was that I flirted a little. That wouldn't break me.

We clinked glasses, then did the two shots. At once. On an empty stomach. I already felt it hitting me as my hand was grabbed and my scantily clad body was hurled onto the dance floor.

Song after horrible song blasted at us. But as we laughed and danced around, it felt like entering an alternate dimension. It was silly. Wonderful. Completely freeing.

Kelly and I twirled under the flashing lights, while I tried to take a good look at the men around me. One guy in a dark blue shirt had incredible cheekbones. His jawline looked like it had been sculpted by a portrait artist. He was gorgeous to stare at, and probably would have made a small fortune modeling.

Smiling to myself, I was just happy that I could see the beauty in a man without the heartache for once.

Spinning the other way, I saw Kelly doing a little bump and grind with a bearded guy who was obviously instantly smitten with her. He was an absolute hunk, but I also saw the way he was gentle with her, taking her hand to give her a spin.

Kelly and I had a long-standing agreement that we did not drink to the point of being helpless. If either of us picked up and disappeared, we would send a text to say that we were safe. From the way she was snuggling into that guy's arms right there on the dance floor, I could already tell I would be getting one of those texts later tonight.

The club was so packed that it didn't matter that I was dancing with myself now. A song I actually knew came on, even though it was the strange thumping dance heavy remix.

My arms shot into the air, my hips swiveled, and I let myself go. I found myself smiling, and making tiny patterns with my hips. For the first time in ages, I became lost in the physical sensation of fun. I probably looked drunk, even though I'd only had two. But sometimes my favorite drink made me high more than tipsy.

Just when I was thinking another shot of tequila might be in order, I felt a prickle behind me, as if someone was staring. I spun around, stumbling in my heels. Strong hands gripped my waist, as I looked up into the most mysteriously dark, sexy eyes I'd ever seen.

He smiled, then held his hands up in front of him as if to say that he was sorry for grabbing me.

I mouthed the word, "Thanks," then took a careful look at this guy. He was utterly gorgeous. Tall, and quite broad through the shoulders. His black button-down shirt was a bit snug across his obviously muscular chest. Something about him almost seemed otherworldly. Those deep eyes were already pulling me in.

He cocked his head, obviously checking me out as well. Then he nodded, giving me an incredible grin. Holding out his hand, I took it automatically. Pulling me in, he clasped my hand, lifting it up while holding me tightly around the waist with his other arm. Nobody gave us a second look as we began slow dancing.

His deep voice purred in my ear, "I was dragged here for my friend's birthday, and now I think I need to get him a better gift to thank him." His hand pressed against my lower back. "I love being in the right place at the right time, don't you?"

Looking up at him, the red lights reflected in his eyes, making his grin extra naughty. Dropping my hand, his fingers tangled into the back of my hair. My hands circled his huge shoulders, feeling his heat right through his shirt.

He was hot. Wildly, wickedly hot. And he was looking at me as if he wanted to eat me alive.

Time seemed to slow down. A choice floated before me.

I could be the timid, shy girl I always was. I could blush, and run away. I could dream about the amazing hot hunk who seemed to like me.

Or I could take him. Stretching up, I brought my lips near his, signaling precisely what I wanted. His eyes blazed, then his mouth barely brushed against mine. I moved with him, gliding my lips against his in a feather-light tease. We both shuddered, and he held me tighter.

"You're delicious," he murmured against my lips.

"You should taste me when I've been drinking blue beaches," I giggled. "My tongue would be blue but I'd taste like sugar."

"What are you drinking tonight?"

"Tequila." Then I hiccuped twice.

He laughed, slipping an arm around me to whisper in my ear, "You know, they say that's the devil's drink. Let's get you some water." He led us to the end of the bar that had a water pitcher, and poured for me.

Although I didn't require babysitting, it was sweet that he wanted to take care of me. After a half glass of water, and managing to only splash a tiny bit on the front of my rather low cut dress, the hiccups stopped.

I saw his eyes tracking my lips. "What?" I asked. "Did I smudge my lip gloss?" How was I able to speak with him so normally? I was always so timid around men. Oh right, the booze. Tequila is a chatty drink.

Lifting his hand, he cupped my face while running his thumb along my bottom lip. His mouth came closer, as my eyes riveted to those perfect, full lips. Then he swerved to my ear again to breathe, "It's causing me physical pain to not really kiss you hard right now."

Wrapping my arm around his back, I press my body against his. My other hand began to wander across his chest, the front of his shoulders. Good grief, he must work out a lot. Or work construction or something. The layers of muscle simply added to his insanely attractive physique.

Looking up into those hypnotic dark eyes, I asked, "Why on earth would a guy as gorgeous as you want to kiss someone like me?"

In my tipsy haze, it was a perfectly reasonable question. But he looked at me like I was nuts.

"Beautiful, I couldn't think of a single man in this entire place that wouldn't want you." He paused. "Okay, I did see two guys dancing close together in the corner. You might not be their type. Ninety-nine percent of the guys at this club would gladly switch places with me."

Stretching up, I tipped my chin so that our mouths were only an inch apart. "Maybe you should kiss me then, instead of holding yourself back." I blinked hard, not believing I'd just said that.

His gaze filled with hunger as he stared from my eyes to my lips. "You luscious little temptress," he smiled. "I know that I'm a bad man, but I can't take advantage of a drunk girl."

I raised a finger to tweak his nose. "For the record, I am not drunk. Very slightly tipsy."

He pulled me tighter, as we began to sway again to the terrible music. "It sounds like you would rather I were a bad man than a good man."

"Actually," I said, trying desperately to sound logical, "It would make you a very good man. I am pretty sure that a hard kiss from you would be healing. Therapeutic."

His thick eyebrow raised in a smirk. "How so?"

"The last man who kissed me was bad. Very, very bad. Evil, actually. So, you'd be helping to burn him out of my mind. That's healthy. Right?"

"Mmm, intriguing," he purred into my ear. Then the tip of his tongue tapped the edge of my earlobe and a deep, hot tremor ran through me. "Tell me, as your new therapist, I need to know how long it's been."

"Six months," I confessed.

"No..." he drawled, staring at me as if I were a buffet and he was starving. Nobody had ever looked at me like that, and it was disturbing how much I enjoyed it. "You could not have been single for six whole months. The vultures would have swooped in."

I shook my head, then immediately wished that I hadn't, since a few things were a tiny bit fuzzy around the edges. "No swooping. There has been no swooping at all."

His hand began stroking my lower back in firm circles as he held me. "Poor little kitten. Have you been lonely?" I nodded carefully.

Cupping my face again, his thumb teased my bottom lip until I could barely hold back a whimper. I'd never needed to kiss a man so badly in my life, and he was going to make me snap if he didn't do it soon.

"Has this gorgeous little treasure needed some affection?"

I nodded again. Oh god, he smelled woodsy and fresh. So masculine. So right. His firm hand slid up my spine to nestle in the back of my hair. He spun so that he leaned against the wall, pulling me to him.

"If you want something, sweetheart, I think it would do you a world of good to just take it."

Somehow, that statement was like a bucket of cold water. Terrifying for a split second, then invigorating. Why shouldn't I kiss him first? He obviously wanted me to. Then I realized that if I started it, he didn't have to feel guilty about taking advantage of a tipsy girl.

Before I could overthink everything in the entire world to pieces any more, I stretched up, pressing my lips firmly to his. His arms tightened, pulling me close as we both seemed to fall into another dimension.

There were now two realms of existence. Reality, and kissing this man. His mouth was so warm, soft. My lips parted slightly, and his followed. I felt the touch of his tongue and wasn't even embarrassed by my audible moan. Flames were licking up the backs of my thighs, and my hips shamelessly pressed to his.

I didn't want to ever leave this new world, opening myself completely as our bodies dissolved into each other. The spark I felt everywhere he touched me was almost dangerous, and I would have done anything for more. Anything.

I felt like a new person. His kisses were energizing. Powerful. I could have cried in relief at finding this new existence where everything was soft and warm and he held me so close.

In this deafening, fast-moving place, we were nearly perfectly still. He was so gentle, slowly moving his lips against mine as he nudged our bodies together. My nipples tightened against the heat of his shirt, and I felt him stirring between our hips.

I had no idea how long we slowly kissed while people bounced around us. It was a strange dreamworld. Then some rude person grabbed my arm, shaking me.

Starting to glare, I saw that it was Kelly, holding another shot for me. The man released me, but I liked the way he kept a hand on my hip, almost possessively.

Slamming the shot in a split second, I handed her back the glass as she leaned in to tell me, "I'm so fucking proud of you right now! Go for it." Then she pranced away to meet back up with the bearded guy over by the bar.

The hand on my hip guided me to the back of the room, away from the lights to a darker corner with couches. It was still busy, but it was easier to hear.

"I'm Eric," he murmured against my ear. The way his lips brushed against my skin was so seductive.

"Eden."

His deep eyes crinkled slightly as he grinned. "Yes, being with you is paradise, but what's your name?"

Laughing, I teasingly slapped his shoulder, then my hand ran down his chest. Cheese and crackers, this dude worked out.

But instead of kissing me again, he just wrapped his arms around me. "I'm sorry, I shouldn't be kissing you," he murmured. "That whole total strangers thing." Then he chuckled. "Even though your friend is... what did she say? So fucking proud of you?"

I shook my head, giggling. Then he gently cupped my chin, turning my head up to look at him. "Tell me why she's so fucking proud," he said.

It felt like a command, and I was confused as to why it sent yet another wave of raw lust through me.

"Um, I'm usually really shy around men. So, she's so... darn proud of me for dancing with someone, I guess."

His dark eyes blazed. "Say the word 'fuck' for me."

"No."

Eric howled with laughter, but it wasn't mean spirited in the slightest. "What do you say when you stub your toe?"

"Son of a pirate. Or maybe, sassafras."

"Are you a nun?"

I giggled, my body pulling to his a bit more. "My grandmother taught me that ladies don't curse. Then I was a babysitter for a while when I was seventeen, and the kids had completely foul mouths. I taught them to make up funnier curses, because making people laugh is always better than being crass. Also, I'm studying English, and writing, so I should have a varied vocabulary."

He looked at me in wonder. "You're absolutely adorable."

We were swaying slightly to the awful music, and I felt a wild adrenaline rush brewing in the pit of my stomach. Or, more likely, it was the third shot. I usually stopped at two, but this extra kick was helping me speak openly to him.

"Tell me to stop kissing you," Eric whispered into my ear. Then he kissed down the side of my neck.

"No, don't stop."

His hands gripped my back tighter, one of them slipping a little too low, almost cupping my rear. "Tell me to stop fondling you," he murmured.

"No."

There was electricity flowing back and forth between the two of us. I actually wondered if it was visible if anyone happened to have one of those electric field special cameras that photographed plant auras.

I was falling for him too hard, too fast. Everything about him turned me on. Then he finally brought his mouth to mine again, slow and soft as a whisper.

Eric walked us backward to a couch and we sprawled on it, our lips never parting. We were obviously in a place where we couldn't go any further, which made secret little touches even more sensual. His hand brushed along the bottom curve of my breast, making me moan into his mouth. He pulled me to sit in his lap. I unfastened two buttons on his shirt to loosen it so that I could reach in and run my hands over those shoulders.

My thigh was pressing against his crotch, and I couldn't

resist moving back and forth, teasing him. His eyes blazed again, then he groaned against me. "You're so sexy. You're making me think very impure thoughts."

"Good," I whispered, pressing my breasts against his chest and swaying slightly. "Like what?"

His dark voice in my ear made my blood surge. "Like pulling down your dress and wriggling your hot, curvy body right onto my cock so that we could fuck right here."

I laughed, but his eyes were so serious. He grabbed my behind, arranging me so that I was straddling him. He pulled me down so that my legs were spread, panties brushing against... oh my god... I could feel his hot, hard length through his pants.

A deep shudder ran through me, and he immediately murmured into my ear, "Just think about it for a second. Would you do that? Would you fuck a stranger in a club?"

I shook my head, then grinned as I moved my lips against his ear. "A stranger? Never. But you... maybe."

**2**

---

ERIC

** Tell Me **

I never truly believed in heaven until this moment. Every single detail of this experience was going to be burned into my mind forever. The way her fingers gripped my shoulders. The way her body rocked against mine so sweetly. Especially the way her lips glided against mine, making me hotter than I'd ever been in my life.

I'd had a few crass bimbos throw themselves at me over the years, and I rarely had the time or energy.

But I'd never been close to a girl so precious. She was somehow demure. Refined. Something about the way she held herself was elegant. I could somehow tell that she had never gone to a bar to pick up a man before. This wasn't like her at all, and I wasn't sure how I could sense it.

She was outside of herself, trying on a new personality. It was adorable watching her try so hard, and push herself. I couldn't begin to wonder what I had done to deserve a beautiful girl like this accidentally ending up in my arms. Now that she was here, I was never going to let her go.

She kissed me as if she was afraid to know what would happen if we ever stopped. We were in a magical bubble outside of the world.

Yet in this incredible moment of perfection, I knew that the bar was going to be cleared any minute. There was absolutely no way I could trust her to get home by herself. I knew she wasn't really drunk, but still, every overprotective urge I'd ever had in my life was nothing compared to what I was feeling for her.

If I sent Eden home in a cab and anything happened to her, I would never, ever forgive myself. I was forced to overstep every polite boundary, and simply take her to my place.

"Come on, gorgeous," I murmured into her perfect lips, puffy from at least half an hour of kissing.

"No," she breathed, "Please... I don't want this to ever end."

My heart skipped a couple of beats, then began to race. She felt it too. "We're going to get you some more water," I said gently, "Then we have to leave."

As she looked up at me, her eyes were a bit hazy. But I knew it wasn't from the booze. We were completely high on each other.

I sat us up, then checked us both to make sure that we had our phones, keys, anything important. Her fingers wound into the back of my hair, pulling my mouth to hers again.

"Sweetie, you are dangerously delicious. Did you know that?"

She shook her head, looking at me with such an innocent glance that I felt heat rush up my spine. I'd never wanted a woman this much in my life.

Taking her hand, I stood up and walked her down the

hall toward the back door. I knew there was always a line of cabs in front of a smaller club around the corner.

"We can't go out there," she murmured, looking a bit worried.

Wrapping an arm around her, I held her against me again. "Why not?"

"We can't let this ever stop," she moaned, wrapping her arms around my shoulders and crushing her lips to mine.

This was beyond a makeout. This felt like soul fusion. Some sort of feverish bonding that would leave us both completely changed.

Without even thinking, I backed her against the wall, lifting her hips so that I could grind us together. Her shaky moan caused that strange possessive energy to burn inside me again. Her legs wrapped around my waist. My hand slid into her dress to caress the perfect silky soft skin of her breast.

The way she was writhing against me, shamelessly rocking us together, I knew that I could have done absolutely anything with her that I wanted. There were almost too many thoughts running through my mind to make sense of it all. Then she looked up at me with the sweetest smile.

"Tell me you feel this," she whispered, her voice wavering slightly. "Tell me I'm not crazy."

"You are crazy. We both are. Yes, I feel this," I murmured as I kissed along the side of her neck to nibble her ear. She quivered, tightening her legs around my hips.

In that split-second, I knew precisely what I needed to do.

**3**

---

EDEN

** Morning Light **

The light was too bright. Too yellow. Snuggling deeper into the pillow and blanket, I had no idea what time it was, but figured I could rest a bit more. My pillow was extra soft, and I was so tired that it felt fluffier. Stretching out my legs, I realized that I must have gone to bed with my dress still on.

The realization that I was not in my own bed rolled over me like a wave. Opening my eyes, I saw that I was in a very nice, large bedroom. Rolling over very slowly, I bumped into a pillow.

There was a line of cushions and pillows down the center of the huge bed. Sitting up, I could see a man snoring gently on the other side. I could only see the side of his face and his shoulder, but he had a t-shirt on.

Lying flat on my back, I closed my eyes and silently thanked the universe for apparently stopping me from doing what I had so desperately wanted to last night.

Sitting up slowly, I saw there was a huge glass of water

on the table beside me, and I quickly drank half of it. There was also a bottle of painkillers and a small plate of crackers. My heart lurched in joy. This was definitely the handiwork of a nice man. Someone thoughtful. Or maybe someone used to taking home drunk chicks.

Thank goodness I was not hungover, just a bit tired. Thank goodness I stopped after only a few drinks. I think that small amount of liquor actually made me hyper instead of drunk.

Memories crept around the back of my mind, shooting out little wriggling tentacles of recollection one at a time. We had been kissing in the bar. We had really, seriously been kissing in a hallway. I didn't quite remember how we got here. There was a back alley where we laughed at some purple graffiti. Oh god – we were grinding up against a wall. A cheesy eighties song played in the cab and we sang along.

Looking around the room more carefully, I was impressed. Everything had that minimalist, incredibly posh look to it, like a fancy hotel. Wait – was this a hotel? No, there was a framed photo of a group of people with a dog, and some knick-knacks. Wherever we were, somebody had a very expensive bedroom.

I looked over to see his eyes flutter open, then he rolled to face me.

"Good morning, gorgeous," he murmured.

"Good morning," I smiled. Gesturing to the pillow wall, I laughed, "I guess you think girls have cooties?"

His deep, rumbling laugh was so sexy. "Making out with a tipsy chick is one thing. Especially since you said it was important. No – therapeutic. That was it." His grin was completely disarming. "But I wasn't going to go farther than that. It was so late that I couldn't send you home alone. So I brought you here, and made this pillow fortress so I couldn't reach for you in the night." He chuckled. "I would have taken the couch, but the last time I fell asleep there I really wrenched my neck."

I stared as his line of vision trailed over me. "Yeah," he said softly, "It was very hard not to cuddle you last night."

Sitting up, I tried to give my head a shake as he looked at me. Then I noticed that he was still staring. "What?"

"Holy shit," he breathed. "You should see how devastatingly sexy you look right now."

I laughed, then leaned over, stretching out to look in his dresser mirror. My hair was messy and huge. My eyeliner was smudged in a smoky, sensual way. Maybe it was from only being awake for two minutes, or it could have been the lack of overall sleep. I was a bit paler, making my kiss-bruised lips look dark and full. I looked like I'd just had the wildest sex of my life.

"You look like a rock video vixen," he breathed. "Or the perfect woman vision in a movie."

A tremor ran through me as I turned to see him looking at me with absolute hunger. The muscles of his thick arms tensed as he crawled slowly toward me.

Reaching over the pillow wall, he murmured, "Are you sober enough to allow me to breach the fortress and kiss the princess?" My hand flew to my mouth, knowing that my breath was likely less than fresh. "Don't care," he growled.

In a blink, I was in his arms, his mouth on mine. Feeling his body over me was so seductive that I felt my hips begin to move up against him.

Then just as suddenly, he pulled back. "Sorry," he muttered. "I know we need water and coffee and proper names and all that, but damn..." His eyes raked over me again. "You're so hot I need to eat you alive."

I had no idea what to say to that. I just knew that I needed him to keep touching me, any way he liked.

I'd never felt this urge to totally surrender to a guy before, and I loved it. There was something primal and raw about wanting him to just take me. The tiny whimper that came from my throat was a complete accident, but I felt him shudder.

Then he stopped, pulling back to lock his dark eyes on mine. "I'm going to attempt to be a good host now, and make sure that you're wide awake before making any rash decisions."

"But–"

He jumped up, pulling track pants over his shorts while I snuck a look at those toned thighs and tight ass.

As he passed me on the way to the door, he grabbed my foot through the blanket, giving it a shake. "You drink coffee?"

"Yes."

"Then you know that I should be serving you coffee instead of jumping you when you're hungover. Take your time getting ready. Help yourself to anything in the closet."

Good grief.

This man was incredibly frustrating, but I shouldn't be upset at him for behaving like a gentleman. It wasn't his fault that my libido had apparently completely awoken for the first time last night. Well, it was his fault, but not something I could blame him for.

Hearing him puttering around in the kitchen, I went to his gigantic washroom to scrub my face, run my fingers through my hair, and use his mouthwash. My dress wasn't that inappropriate, so I thought it would probably do for breakfast.

When I went back to his room, I couldn't resist sneaking

a look in his closet. There was a row of sharp suits, mostly in black, with a couple in navy and dark gray. From the look of his wardrobe, and the way this place was decorated, he was obviously extremely well off.

Padding barefoot down the hall, I could smell coffee, and Eric was starting to cook something on the stove. I couldn't resist walking straight to the giant floor to ceiling living room window that looked across half of the city.

"Wow," I breathed.

Eric's bright chuckle came from behind me, then echoed through the room. "Yeah, that's why I bought this place. I love watching the city wake up. Or go to sleep. Or just hang out."

After staring across the concrete and glass expense for a few minutes, I came over to the breakfast bar just as Eric slid a mug in front of me. "Milk or cream?"

"Either one is fine."

He set milk, cream, sugar, and a spoon in front of me, then went back to cutting thick slices of bread.

Watching the graceful way he moved was absolutely hypnotic. Even the way he skimmed the spatula around the giant frying pan was sort of a slow dance.

Taking a sip of coffee, I almost moaned. "Holy squid, this is amazing."

His sexy grin made my fingers twitch around the mug. "It's a secret blend I've been working on over the years."

"Would it be rude to ask how old you are?" I asked.

He waved the spatula at me. "Yes. But I'm thirty-seven. Does that matter?"

I shook my head emphatically. "Not at all."

Eric looked me up and down with a smirk. "I'm guessing you're... twenty-six-ish?"

"Um, twenty-four."

He stared at the utensil in his hand. "That's pretty young. Do I care about that?" he asked the spatula. "Nah, she seems really mature. And calm. Most younger girls are flighty." He nodded. "She muttered something about studying last night, so she's still in school. She seems smart."

Dropping his chin, he faced me. "We're good."

I nearly spilled my coffee, I was laughing so hard.

**4**

---

ERIC

** Brunch **

I'd always loved cooking for people, but didn't have many opportunities. I didn't date much, and until last night, I'd never taken a woman home on a whim.

Occasionally I've cooked for my sister Angie, or a couple of University buddies. I once cooked for my assistant when we had to work all weekend on a project, and the air-conditioning in the office was sketchy. I think it was one of the very few times I've actually surprised Patricia. Maybe even impressed her.

Cooking was something that usually held my focus, sort of a meditative task. But this morning it was hard to concentrate. I couldn't stop sneaking looks at the way Eden was smiling into her mug.

She was exquisitely beautiful, but it was so much more than that. Outwardly, she was fairly normal. She had a healthy, curvy figure with very shapely legs. The way she tossed her long brown hair around expressively made tiny reddish highlights stand out.

There was also a sense of deep quiet around her. As if she wasn't sure she belonged out in the world or not. There was a delicate softness to her shy energy that I found fascinating.

How strange that I was absolutely taken with this adorable girl, and I didn't know a thing about her.

"So, what do you do?" I asked her.

"I'm studying English, writing, with a few media courses," she said.

"Cool. Where do you intend to go with that?"

Her sweet laugh rang out, and I looked over to see her warm brown eyes smiling at me. "I guess that's the million-dollar question," she said. "The theory is, with a broad education, I can go into anything, and follow the market. People always need writers, right?"

I nodded. "We certainly do."

"I want enough of a background so that I could write advertising copy, educational textbooks, or even ghostwrite terrible biographies for nonsense celebrities."

I chuckled. "Not keeping all your eggs in one basket. That's wise."

Her head tilted and she looked absolutely delighted by what I said. "My Nana always says that," she said.

"Then she is a wise lady," I said, flipping the eggs carefully. Then I fired her a glance from the corner of my eye. "Just a little warning, I like smart chicks."

"Chick?" she asked haughtily, then she giggled. "Yes, I know all girls in their early twenties get lumped into one category."

I shook my head, sliding the omelets onto two plates and adding slices of thick, buttery toast. "Not at all. I've seen a lot of women at all ages who are complete flakes, and a few who were extremely driven." I slid a plate in front of her.

"But the same could be said for men. The only difference is the terminology. Women are chicks and flakes, whereas men are bros and sportos. Often douchebags. There doesn't seem to be a convenient term for people who work hard, have a steady life, and like having a few routines."

"Regular people?" she suggested. "That just sounds boring as beans."

I set out cutlery and a linen napkin, and Eden looked extremely impressed. "This is amazing, thank you," she said.

"You're very welcome," I said, sitting on the stool beside her.

"What do you do?" she asked.

I swallowed a bite of my toast before answering. "You know those little boys who love building things with their blocks? The ones who make towers that are bigger and bigger every time?"

Eden nodded. "Yeah."

"That's me. I liked it so much that I worked construction, then went to university to study engineering. I'm lucky enough to have a sister who is a financial and planning genius. So between the two of us, we own Two Stones. We assemble the people and teams who make buildings, and oversee the projects."

"Wow," she said softly. "You're the head of the company?"

"I'm the CEO. Angie is the CFO." Her eyes were wide, and I didn't want to sound like I was bragging. "The two of us have both concentrated on hiring people who are smarter than us, so the head of every division is a star in their own way. That helped the company grow a bit faster than it should have, actually."

She grinned. "Do you still play with blocks?"

I laughed. "As a matter of fact, I really do. We just had a rough wooden scale model of Toronto constructed so that everyone can visualize different buildings and how they will affect what's around them."

"I'd love to see that," she said softly.

"Anytime."

She was already pushing her plate away. "That was incredible. I'm stuffed. Thank you so much."

Her eyes were bright and clear, and she looked so delicious that I knew I couldn't resist her any longer. "Are you hungover at all?" I asked, trying not to leer.

"Not in the slightest."

"You've had enough coffee that you would consider yourself wide awake?"

"Yes." Her eyebrow raised slightly as she realized I was getting at something, but she didn't know what.

Pushing my plate away, I stood up and dabbed my mouth with the napkin. Taking her hand, I led her to the empty end of the kitchen island, wrapping my hands around her waist as I pulled her against me. "There's something I've been craving for a long time, and I wondered if you could help me."

Brushing my thumb along her bottom lip, she nodded slowly. "Anything."

It thrilled me to see how aroused she was just from standing pressed against me. I kissed her gently, her supple lips moving softly under mine, driving us both wild. I could feel a tremor run through her as my hand slid down to grip her ass firmly.

"I'm still hungry," I said, surprised at the dark tone of my voice.

"Tell me what you need," she purred.

Grabbing the hem of her dress, I started pulling it up very slowly, while watching her soft eyes. She bit her lip shyly, but gave me a nod. Pulling it off completely, I had known that she wasn't wearing a bra from how thin the fabric was. But her little red lace panties were the perfect mix of seductive and sweet. Taking a step back, I stared at her lovely soft skin. "Breathtaking," I whispered, making her blush.

Skimming my fingers around her waistband, I began to pull them down very slowly. "Once you're naked, I'm going to put you up on the counter, and eat your sweet pussy until I am completely satisfied. What do you think of that?"

She looked like she was twitching, fluttering slightly from head to toe. Pulling her against me, I breathed into her ear, "I think I'm going to need to hear you say 'no', or 'fuck yes'."

She looked up at me, then suddenly gripped the back of my neck, kissing me hard. I couldn't believe the heat rolling off of this gorgeous girl.

"Yes," she said softly.

"Close enough."

Pulling her panties off, I lifted her onto the counter, loving her squeal as her butt hit the chilly marble. Spreading her legs, I reached up to caress her breasts while kissing the inside of her knees, turning my head back and forth.

I loved the feeling of her nipples turning into tight peaks under my thumb as I moved from one side to the other. I adored her gasps as I kissed up her inner thighs.

I stared at her naked pink pussy, so open and inviting. I'd always thought it was a beautiful thing when a woman opened herself to a man. I knew that she must have felt nervous, vulnerable, and likely curious as well. Yet she was allowing me to play with her so intimately.

Instead of moving higher, I worked lower, all the way down to her ankle bone before skimming my lips slowly all the way back up to her inner thigh. Grazing my tongue along the seam where her leg met her body, I heard her soft sigh.

"You look so precious laid out for me like a buffet, gorgeous," I murmured.

"I love the way you touch me," she whispered.

Her hips wriggled slightly, and I could feel that she was getting impatient. Spreading her labia gently with my thumbs, her soft, delicate pussy was imprinting on my memory as my new favorite vision. Examining her carefully, I flattened my tongue against her little nub of nerves, licking her slow and steady while she moaned softly.

Circling her pussy lips with my finger, I nudged in very slightly. She was already hot and slippery, and it felt like her tunnel was trying to pull my finger in. Thrusting slowly and carefully, I glided inside her.

It sounded like her breath was hitching, already slightly ragged. Feeling her thighs quiver around my ears made my pulse race, as I flicked my tongue over her swollen clit over and over.

I added a second finger to her pulsing pussy, gliding slow and deep through her softness. Circling her clit with my tongue, her desperate moans were making me harder than I'd ever been before.

But I was focused on her pleasure, not mine. Pinching her nipple slightly, I worked my fingers a bit faster, licking her clit again in sharp upward strokes.

Eden began to fall to pieces under my touch. Her fingers gripped the back of my shoulders, as I heard her whisper, "Oh fuck... Fuck, Christ, don't stop."

I worked her hot body harder and faster, loving the sensation as she tipped over the edge into a squirming, squealing animal as she climaxed.

She whispered so softly it was barely a breath, "Fucking hell."

I slowed my pace as her whispered curses turned back into soft moans. Then I stood up straight, keeping a hand on her belly so she wouldn't try to roll and fall off the counter. I kissed her almost roughly, so she could feel the heat that was surging through me.

Her eyes were wide. "I had no idea," she blurted.

"Oh my god... Baby, has no one done that for you before?"

She shook her head, a wave of shyness overtaking her again. "I've... You know. Done some things. Just not that."

I kissed her again, deep and soft as her lips opened for mine. Her tongue was so soft and wet against mine. We moved together so naturally that everything we did felt right.

Finally I pulled her against me, helping her slide off the counter to stand. Holding her body to mine, I wondered whether I should push my luck.

**5**

----

EDEN

** Falling Water **

I felt so strange. Like I was floating, even as Eric held me still. It felt so perfect and natural to have his body pressed against mine.

I couldn't even believe that I met him less than twelve hours ago. It felt right to be so close to him. It was shocking that I let him lick me like that without a second thought. It was so intimate and raw that I knew it would take me a couple of days to process that experience completely.

My ex would never consider doing such a thing. Now that I thought about it, I wasn't sure whether I would have trusted him. Yet I trusted Eric completely. Every time he touched me, it was a magical blend of sweet possession, balanced with consideration, and what seemed to be a deep urge to bring me pleasure.

"That was amazing," I said gently, looking up at him. I felt dazed, and wondered if he could see stars in my eyes.

"I hope you don't have to leave yet," he said, gripping my

waist and swaying my body against his as if we were dancing again. "Are you a good environmentalist?"

That question came out of nowhere. "I try?"

"We should all try to conserve water," he murmured against my hair, our rocking back and forth gathering energy. "It would be very environmentally responsible of us to take a shower together."

A deep ache pulled my hips low just thinking about his huge body completely naked, splashed with water. Then I realized what else would certainly happen while we were in there.

My body wanted him completely. No, needed him. Not to cleanse my palate and help me move on from the ex. I needed him for myself. I didn't even know whether or not there was a possibility of a relationship here, and it didn't matter.

Honestly, he had the most important things covered already. He was sweet to me, he listened to me, and he was a responsible, contributing member of society.

The basics were pretty basic, but Kelly and I had agreed that some very simple ground rules should be in place before we ever considered dating a guy. Or being naked with a guy. The list was brought about due to Kelly's penchant for dating musicians who were always begging for rent money and food.

Eric seemed to have it all together. But for me, the most important thing was that he really listened. He seemed to always be checking in with both my words and my body language. It was refreshing. He was actually a gentleman. But now I needed to know what it felt like when he acted more like an animal.

I nodded very seriously. "Yes, conserving water is very

important. We should definitely have a shower before we get back to our regular lives."

Eric stopped moving, cupping my face in his. "I don't want my regular life unless you're in it."

My mouth fell open, but I couldn't speak, just nodding.

"I'm serious," he said gently, kissing across my forehead, then down the edge of my cheek. "I don't care that we met in a cheesy dance club. We can figure out the details when we get to know each other better. But this is not a one time thing, right?"

I nodded quickly and eagerly, still unable to form words.

His grin made me feel weightless, floating again. "I'm going to need you to speak out loud again. You say, 'Yes, I want you to take me into the shower and have wet, naughty sex with me until I scream with joy'."

My eyes clamped shut as I laughed, feeling how hard I was blushing. "Yes," I managed to whisper. "Shower, and... stuff."

He picked me up, and I automatically wrapped my legs around his waist. How on earth was I comfortable being naked while he was fully clothed?

Walking slowly to the bedroom, he peppered my neck with kisses while murmuring, "Try again. Say, 'I need you to fuck me in the shower'." I moaned as his lips wandered down to my nipple. Carrying me through the bedroom, he leaned me against the wall of the bathroom.

"Say it," he nearly growled, his dark eyes almost aggressive.

"Yes. Shower sex," I managed to mumble.

His teeth latched onto my collarbone and he gave me a tiny bite, making me yelp. "See? You can be louder," he grinned. "We'll work on that."

He started the shower, adjusting the water for both the

overhead rain attachment and a dozen side jets. The thing looked so complicated there was probably an online course on how to work it. Then Eric peeled his t-shirt off, and I forgot how to breathe.

I'd never seen a body like that up close. The layers of muscle across his chest, his ribs, down his chiseled stomach. His thick arms and broad, rounded shoulders. It was mind blowing.

His eyes twinkled with a touch of pride. "I like the gym," he shrugged. "And rock climbing."

I turned away to step into the water, but my head twisted back to watch as he slid off his track pants and shorts. Wow. His legs were a work of art, but I could barely see them from the distraction of what was swinging between them.

His shaft was long, thick, and looked absolutely sculpted. It looked like a model for sex toys. And I was pretty sure it was only half hard.

Tossing his clothes aside, he came into the shower, immediately pressing me up against the wall for a long, deep kiss. Then he stared at me, taking in my pale skin as the water glided over me. I knew that I was standing as if I was terrified for him to touch me.

He seemed to read me immediately, hugging me in a way that would be platonic if we weren't naked in a shower. "You were so wild and free with a bit of booze dashing around inside you. Can't you do the same for me with coffee? Can't you show me that wild girl who couldn't keep her hands off me?"

Maybe he didn't mean for it to sound like a dare, but I couldn't help my reaction. My hands slid around his waist to grab his tight ass, pulling his hips to mine. "This is an amazing shower," I smiled.

"Yeah, I've always wanted to have a girl in here," he said, pumping a tiny bit of liquid soap into his hands.

He began caressing my breasts, sliding them together, then gliding over every inch. "You were shaking these a bit on the dance floor," he said quite seriously. "So we'd better make sure that they are absolutely clean now."

Reaching out to take a little soap as well, I begin to scrub his shoulders and chest. I loved the way he seemed to tremble slightly from the feeling of my hands moving quickly across his skin. I couldn't believe that I was affecting him as much as he was thrilling me.

Eric turned me to face the wall, his hands brushing my hair over my shoulder as he kissed down my spine. I loved the way he manhandled me so gently. It was confident. Unnervingly sexy.

He carefully pulled my hips away from the wall, spreading my legs. My hands grabbed at the tiles for balance as he dropped to his knees, spreading me open. The long, languid strokes of his tongue under the falling water were almost too much to take.

I was overwhelmed. Overheated. The need to have him inside me was becoming almost painful.

"Please," I whispered, the sound almost lost under the sounds of the falling water.

"Please what?" he murmured against my clit.

"I need you," I gasped.

"Mmm..." He moaned as he increased his pace, licking steadily. "What do you need?" he mumbled.

"You," I breathed.

"You already have me. I'm right here."

Son of a... He was going to make me say it. Somehow the way he was gently pushing for me to say things out loud was a strange turn on. Like he was controlling me in a very subtle way, but it was obviously for my own good.

"I need you inside me," I whispered.

Immediately he stood up, spinning me so my back was against the wall again. His eyes burned to mine. "Should I go get a condom?"

I shook my head, water falling into my eyes. "I'm on the pill."

He lifted my hips so that I could wrap my legs around his waist. Reaching out, I touched his shaft carefully, stroking along his hot length. His expression softened as I touched him, as if he couldn't believe this was happening. I certainly couldn't.

I stroked him gently, not able to imagine it getting harder, then pulled the thick, round head to my opening. I was incredibly wet, yet he still took his time. Running the tip through my pussy lips over and over, I realized he was teasing me. I began to squirm, my body desperate for his.

Then he nudged at my opening, sinking inside just a little bit. "Is this what you want, baby?"

"Yes. More."

"I want to hear you say it," he grinned. "I get that you are a shy, polite young lady. But I really want to hear you say it. 'Eric, I want to feel your cock inside me'. You can do it."

He stared into my eyes while rocking the tip of his shaft inside me just half an inch. The steamy water all around us was making everything seem like a dream. He was about to give me everything I wanted. The least I could do was give him what he asked for.

Gripping the back of his neck, I pulled his ear to my lips. "I need your cock inside me, please," I breathed. Instantly he began sinking inside me, so hard and thick and perfect. I gasped as he filled me completely, feeling my body stretch around his width.

Yet he didn't fuck me.

The deep, hypnotic rhythm of his shaft pulling all the way out, stroking all the way in. This was lovemaking. This was absolutely beautiful. It was so intense that I felt tears prick my eyes.

Although my nervous system was overloaded, there was something deep and peaceful about the way he moved inside me. He was touching every nerve, and the base of his shaft rubbed against my clit with every stroke. He grabbed my ass so firmly that I had no fear of falling, as my hips swiveled against his.

My head fell forward against his shoulder, and I heard my voice cry out, "Oh fuck, yes."

"Tell me how it feels," Eric growled against my ear. He was nearly panting, and it felt like he was holding back.

"Mind blowing," I breathed. "I've never been this full of cock. I've never felt anyone control me the way you do."

"I don't want to control you, Eden," he said sweetly, "I just want to bring you out of your shell and be a bit louder. That's all."

Then he kissed me. There was something different in this kiss. Something about the way he pressed his body into mine, his tongue into my mouth, his hands supporting my body completely. He was claiming me. I was utterly his in every way. It felt like he took this responsibility seriously, as if he deeply wanted to care for me while I was under his power.

The rhythm of his hard, thick length moving against my inner muscles, grinding against my clit, was causing a prickling wave to surge through me.

"Mmm," Eric smiled through our infinite kiss. "Is my gorgeous little treasure going to come for me?"

I nodded, my head rolling against the tile behind me.

"Say it, baby," he begged.

I looked at him, wide-eyed. "Does it turn you on when I talk dirty?"

He nodded eagerly, grinning. "You don't say bad words, so I need to hear them."

He held me close again, thrusting deeper, faster. His blend of tenderness and sexy cockiness was pushing me over the edge as much as all of these incredible physical sensations. We were both so close, and I could feel his throbbing length swelling inside me.

"Say it," he growled. "Tell me how much you want to come."

The rippling waves were starting, and I was already past the point of no return.

"Oh fuck," I breathed against his ear, my fingernails digging into the back of his shoulders as I quaked. "I'm coming... coming all over your cock. Is that what you need to hear? Oh fuck... Fuck me harder." Orange lights hovered around the edge of my vision as I dissolved into the heat-wave of the impossibly perfect climax.

Eric exploded with an unearthly growl, grinding up into me hard and rough as his hot release burst inside me. I was trembling from head to toe, moaning and twitching uncontrollably.

He held me still for several breaths, then helped me stand back on the floor. It was sweet the way he kept an arm around me, not quite trusting my balance yet.

He looked down at me, his wide eyes serious. "Eden," he choked, kissing me gently, "That was..." I nodded quickly, sinking into his kiss as I wrapped my fingers into the back of his hair.

Then he stepped back, laughing brightly. "Oh right. We were supposed to be getting clean."

He swept me back until I was leaning over his arm so that he could tenderly rinse between my legs with the falling water. I began giggling, feeling almost high from his endless caresses.

He laughed while I washed his hair. I giggled while he scrubbed my back. It was so relaxed and light. Comfortable.

When he finally turned all the water jets off, wrapping me in a fluffy robe, I was surprised when he led us out to the living room. "Another coffee?"

"Sure."

# 6

---

ERIC



I'd honestly never slept with a total stranger. It was debaucherous, indulgent, and so perfect. The thing that tempered the naughtiness was knowing that it wasn't a one time thing. There was no way we weren't about to become a couple. I could feel that we were meant to be.

Walking Eden to the kitchen, both of us wrapped in robes, I could envision us living together someday. Being like this all the time.

I spun her into my arms, kissing the top of her damp hair. Holding her against me, I felt a prickle run up my spine. I had real feelings for Eden. Big, sloppy feelings that had nothing to do with lust. Well, a few bits, but only because it made me feel so close to her.

Closing my eyes for a moment, I tried to breathe. If I took a lie detector test at this moment and was asked if I loved her, the needle would tweak. I was already falling very hard.

Snapping my eyes open, Eden was staring at me. I reached out to caress her cheekbone with my thumb.

"I've never slept with anyone that I haven't been dating for at least a month," I confessed. "So I hope it's okay if we do things a little backward. First, we slept together, then we..." I waggled my eyebrows. "Slept together." She giggled. "May I take you out to dinner this week?" I asked.

She nodded. Then she glanced at the clock and winced. "Oh, I'll have to skip the coffee. I'm sorry I have to go. I have to do all of that boring Sunday stuff like laundry and groceries and everything that keeps me alive through the week."

She picked up her panties and dress from the kitchen floor, then dashed to the bedroom to get dressed. I wanted to work on her shyness until we were prancing around naked all the time. Glancing across the living room, I made a mental note to consider drawing the curtains first.

Eden came back out with her purse in hand. "Hold on," I said. I went to the hall closet and grabbed an oversized hoodie for her to wear over her thin dress.

"Thanks." She pulled it on and zipped it up, flashing me that adorable smile. It was amusing that I thought she looked sexier in my lumpy gray hoodie than her little red dress.

"Can I get your number?" I asked.

"Sure."

We traded phones to exchange numbers, but she looked surprised when I handed hers back. "Erlik? I thought you said Eric?"

I shrugged. "I've always gone by Eric. I just typed that in case you had any other Eric in your phone." Suddenly I felt weird. Almost nervous. "Funny – I never tell anyone my real name." I smiled at her. "Proof that you're special, I guess."

Eden stared into space for a second, then shook her head. "I don't think I've heard that name before. Where is it from?"

I rolled my eyes. "Please don't judge me. My parents were weird punk-ass hippies. They thought that giving me a name that meant 'a deity of darkness' would make me tough or something." I chuckled. "You've witnessed my finesse at making omelets, so you know I have a fluffy side as well, right?"

Eden laughed, but it didn't touch her eyes. "Deity of darkness?" She looked a bit queasy.

"Yeah. The underworld. Erlik is a demon, apparently."

"The devil." Her whisper sounded harsh. Strained.

"You can call me Eric," I said quickly. She honestly looked upset. "Dammit, I'm sorry. My parents are weirdos, but they're not Satanists or anything super dark. They meant it like a force of nature, I think." Desperately trying to grin, I said, "Your name is the original paradise. So we balance each other. Right?"

Eden smiled and nodded, but she was stiff. "Well, thanks for taking such great care of me. I'll see you around."

"Hey," I said gently, pulling her into my arms. She felt so incredible against me, as if her body was designed to mold into mine. "Send me a text so that I know you're home safe?"

She nodded against my chest as I stroked her hair. Leaning down for a tiny kiss, she seemed to be quivering. Tipping her chin up with my finger, I tried to make her smile. "I can't wait to have dinner with you. I bet you have some weird family stories as well."

She nodded, then dashed out. I sunk onto the couch, dumbfounded.

Was she shy after the most amazing sex of my life? There was no way she couldn't have felt that connection.

Was it the process of getting her number that made her uneasy? Maybe she assumed this was a one-morning stand situation. I knew she didn't know me very well, but I hoped she didn't think I was that kind of guy. I don't think I did anything to lead her to believe that.

I managed to wait three whole hours before sending her a text.

*Eden, I know I'm supposed to pretend to be cool and wait a few days to text you. I can't play games. I think you're incredible. May I take you out for a proper date this Friday night?*

Four minutes later, not that I was counting and holding my breath, she read the message. I saw the three dots hover as she typed. Then they disappeared. No response.

Maybe she was on the subway. Maybe she picked up groceries on the way home and her hands were full.

Maybe...

There was no way she couldn't want more of what we had?

**7**

———————

EDEN

The deity of the underworld. The devil.

Son of a biscuit. Nana's warning echoed in my ears, in the back of my mind. It was so oddly specific.

"Never get in bed with the devil." There wasn't much room for interpretation about that one.

Laying sprawled across my bed, I stared at the ceiling. Then I nearly cried thinking about how hilarious Eric was when he was chatting so naturally to a spatula.

He was quirky. Silly. I liked that in a hot, strong, hunky guy. A little silliness is underrated. A sense of humor and lightness is important.

"He lives for darkness and fire."

Is there any way Nana could have meant passion? Maybe his passion would be too much for me, and I'd have a great life being slightly overwhelmed?

I wished that I could have a cup of tea with her and ask. Nobody had ever talked to her directly about The Knowing, but would that be bad? She must be aware of it. My sister had been talking about going out to visit Nana in Vancouver in a few months. I had a bit of money saved up. Maybe I could splurge and go as well.

Rolling onto my side, I reached for my journal but didn't bother opening it. I didn't want to fill it with more pages of how scared I was. The pages were already heavy with my nervous rantings. I was much less nervous around Eric. It felt incredible to have my anxiety turned down.

Logically, I knew that on some level I believed in Nana's warning because I was scared of dating again. Dating Eric would be totally different, in more ways than I could likely think of. He was powerful, confident. Gorgeous. He was incredibly sweet. It would be far too easy to hand him the shriveled fragments of my heart and hope that he could breathe life back into it.

But what if he failed.

Sitting up, I grabbed my pen and opened the notebook. There must be something else I could vent about to bring me back to reality.

Then my phone pinged, and I read new texts from Eric.

*Reasons why you might not get back to me:*

*Zombies. Work emergency. Vacation in a hippie commune that doesn't allow cell phones.*

*You live in a complicated apartment where everything is monogrammed with E for Eden, and you're terrified someone named Eric would mess up your system. I'll gladly change my name to see you again. How about Nermal? Or Thornton?*

*If it's something I did wrong, please know I'd do absolutely anything to make it up to you, and be given another chance.*

Son of a pirate. Son of a biscuit. Frick.

I almost laughed at my semi-curses.

Then a tremor ran through me as I remembered what I was saying to Eric in the shower. Good grief. That was so hot. The feeling of those words leaving my mouth, knowing how much he craved them... I shuddered from head to toe just thinking about it.

Nana said that a lady doesn't curse. Even if you're poor as dirt, up to your elbows in wash water, a woman should still behave like a lady. My Mom once said that Nana wouldn't say 'crap' if her mouth were full of it.

Trying to put Nana's warning out of my mind, I thought maybe I should take just a moment to be logical. If I didn't have a grandmother who randomly said semi prophetic things, would I go out with this guy again?

Absolutely. No question.

I opened my laptop and searched for Erlik Stone. There weren't any. I searched for Eric Stone. There were dozens until I added the word "construction". Then there was only one in Toronto.

"Sweet fancy dancers," I muttered.

It turns out that my accidental pick up wasn't just some guy.

Eric had said that he and his sister ran Two Stones – a corporation that oversaw building projects. More specifically, they made incredible office towers all across North America. He really was the head of the company. I didn't think he was lying, but people often exaggerate. If anything, he seriously downplayed his position.

I could tell by his condo and that building that he was obviously wealthy, but this was a bit much to take in. My brain just couldn't absorb it.

I'd never cared much about money, as long as I had enough to take care of myself. It was the power that came with extreme wealth that was a bit strange for me to consider. I searched again until I found a photo attached to the name and title. Yes, that was definitely him.

Slumping onto my bed, I tried not to cry. Staring out the window, it only took about twenty seconds for me to fail spectacularly. Fat tears dripped down my face as I thought about all of the lies and manipulation from my ex, Andy.

In the beginning, I was a bit surprised that he seemed so eager to date me. A month later, I had thought that we really clicked. He was my first real boyfriend in every possible way.

Sure, I didn't like the way he talked down to me, or the way I seemed to be number seven or eight on his list of priority people. But he was usually there for important things.

Then when my Mom was in the hospital, and I needed

him most, I found out the truth. He had been dating me because he was trying to get promoted at work. He thought that since the company was so vocal about their family values that he should have a steady girlfriend to show how wholesome he was.

Using someone to further their career was something that happened in cheesy soap operas. But I overheard him talking to his friend about it.

Andy had gone to get us some coffee while we were in the waiting room of the hospital after my Mom's hip replacement surgery. After a while, I came to look for him, and overheard him on the phone with his dudebro, Chad.

He was going on about how he found a much hotter girl who would be a better fake girlfriend, and then fiancé. He went on to describe their existing sugar baby arrangement that would suit him much better, rather than having to deal with my apparent neediness. But he would wait a day or two to break up with me, since I seemed so worried about my Mom.

The way he had described me made me feel more pathetic, lost, and alone than I ever had in my life. Not exactly what I needed when my Mom was being wheeled into recovery.

I never understood the concept of a broken heart before that day. I thought it was a poetic turn of phrase. Something abstract.

When I discovered the man I thought I'd loved had been using me, and was about to throw me away like trash, my heart didn't break, exactly. It vaporized. It was replaced with a dark, heavy cloud that sat in my chest, poisoning my blood with every breath.

It took six months to be able to look at myself in the mirror without wanting to punch it. It took journaling, kickboxing classes, and endless wine-soaked tear-stained nights with my girlfriends to finally consider putting myself out there again someday.

When I went out dancing with Kelly, I'd finally forced myself to look at men again. I had no way to know that I'd literally stumble into a man who would have been absolutely perfect for me if not for his name.

The universe has a sick, twisted sense of humor about some things.

Now all I could do is avoid Eric, and know that someday, there was hope that my heart might heal enough to let someone in for more than one wild night and morning.

At least there was hope. That was always important.

**8**

---

ERIC

** Desperation **

After sending Eden several texts and not hearing back, I sent her just one a day. Something chatty and light. I didn't want to sound desperate, even though I obviously was.

By Wednesday night I was losing my mind. I didn't want to obsess over her, but I couldn't help it. There was no way I could go back to my regular life. I needed Eden.

Stepping outside of myself, I was fully aware of how nuts that sounded. If a buddy of mine came to me and explained this situation, I'd tell him to try texting her again next week, then let it go and move on.

There was no way in heaven or hell I was going to let Eden go.

I went home from work a bit early to sit in the center of my living room in sweat pants and a tank top, likely looking disheveled and pathetic. My giant sketchpad was always how I brainstormed things. Somehow scribbling and making a mess helped me think.

She didn't even tell me her last name. How could I not have gotten that information? I was normally extremely detail-oriented.

But until she was about to leave, there was zero doubt in my mind that I'd be seeing her again within a day or two.

I shut my eyes and tried to focus. All I could think of was the feeling of her skin. The way she was so polite until we were naked. She seemed so shy at first, then with the slightest encouragement, she blurted out that she needed me.

Holy shit, that was officially the hottest moment of my life. Feeling her surrender to the moment was more satisfying than my own climax, which was mind-scrambling, for the record.

Focus. Serious brainstorm time. It was effective with projects at work. This was much bigger, much more important. What clues did I have that would help me find her?

While we were joking about the dreadful music at the club, she mentioned a band she liked. I looked them up earlier, and they weren't playing in town any time soon.

She mentioned sending a text to her friend Kelly to say that she was safe. I was pretty sure that she didn't go to that dance club often, but I'd go there every Friday and Saturday night until the end of time if that's what it took.

But she didn't seem to really like the music there. She wasn't a party girl. What did she like?

Just picturing her in that little red dress made my heart rate soar. Red. Didn't she say something about a color?

I sat on the floor, trying to concentrate. I didn't know why sitting on the ground always seemed to help. I doodled circles in the margins of the page. Then diamonds. Then arrows. Maybe I should try colored pens instead of a pencil.

Blue. Her tongue would have been blue if she'd been drinking blue beaches.

I'd thought at the time I must have misheard her, but that sounded like a cocktail. It was something.

Grabbing my phone, I made a call that would definitely change my status from a nice guy to a potential stalker, and I didn't care.

"Yes, Mr. Stone?" The crisp voice that answered was the epitome of efficiency.

"Patricia, I am so sorry, but I need to send you on an insane wild goose chase."

I could almost hear her grabbing her ever-present notebook and pen. "Go ahead."

It was freaking hilarious that I could probably have sent my assistant to comparison shop for supercars, pick out women's high heels in my size, or analyze every Chinese food restaurant in the city. She would approach the project with an equal amount of dedication, while pointedly rolling her eyes at me. As she should.

"There is a bar, cocktail lounge, or pub somewhere in the city that serves a drink called a Blue Beach. I need to find out where that is."

There was a long pause. She probably thought I'd gone off the deep end this time. "Is it a central location, sir?"

"Probably. I would start with a two-mile radius around the club district and work out from there."

"Priority?"

I sighed heavily. "Obviously office work comes ahead of this, but I'm sort of desperate."

She paused for a moment. "Sir, the two new interns have been looking for a research project. Shall I give this to them, and make it sound like some sort of test?"

"Perfect," I said. "Give them each a bonus for trying hard, and give the winner something extra."

"I'm on it. Is there anything else?"

"That's it. Thanks, Patricia."

I tried to tell myself it wasn't stalking. I certainly wasn't looking up Eden's home address. Or where she went to school. Did she work as well? I didn't even know.

Standing up and walking to the window, I looked out across the city. The five-year-old part of me loved being higher than most of the other buildings. It made me feel like a superhero. Like somebody who was in control.

Most parts of my life had been fairly controlled. There had been a plan, steps had taken place, and there was an end result. Things almost always worked out. Sure, sometimes there would be added steps in the middle, or something unexpected would happen. But the target was always acquired. The goal was always reached. It was extremely rare that any project in my life was completely abandoned.

I didn't have a lot of experience at failing. I would just try again and again in new and different ways until I got the result I wanted. Or at least something fairly close. This gave me a feeling of power that admittedly, was pretty terrific most of the time

Now I was faced with a challenge that made me feel weak. I didn't know what I'd do if I couldn't find her.

Grabbing my phone, I called up my notes. The things I was jotting down would have made me sick had I seen another guy do it.

Private investigator. Call up security photos from my condo lobby to get her photo. Find a hacker who could figure out her full name and address from her phone number.

Honestly, I didn't want to do any of those things. It was

extremely creepy. If she found out I did something like that, Eden would freak out, and she would be right to do so. I couldn't start a relationship with her like that. It wasn't right.

She was so pure. So full of light. I wanted us to start dating in a nice, normal way. Dinner and a movie. Bowling. One of those escape room adventures.

Unable to stand being awake any longer, I went to bed early, getting up at six am to hit the gym hard. I need to burn out this frustration. I needed my muscles to ache more than my heart did.

I finally dragged myself back up to my condo for a shower and to get dressed for the day. Then I picked out a red tie the exact shade of Eden's dress from Saturday night, just so I could feel like I had a tiny connection to her.

I had officially become sappy.

I went to my office and had a nice, normal morning, even though I couldn't quite distract myself from my misery.

At a quarter to noon, Patricia came in with some paperwork, my second coffee, and a gigantic smile. The first two things were normal. The third was exceedingly rare.

After setting down the coffee and dropping folders full of contracts on my desk, she waved to a sheet of paper on top. "Names and addresses of twenty-three places that serve a Blue Hawaiian or a Blue Lagoon, just in case you were mistaken." Patricia pointed to the name of a pub that was in bold at the top. "And the one place in the city that has a drink called a Blue Beach."

I blinked hard, feeling absolutely paralyzed for several heartbeats.

"Thank you," I said quietly. "Please tell the interns thank you as well. And give them each a three hundred dollar bonus."

"Dare I ask what this is about?" she asked.

Looking up at my assistant, I knew she was about to laugh at me, and that I deserved it. What the hell. "It's to help me find the girl of my dreams," I said frankly.

Her mouth actually fell open. Then she snapped it shut and shook her head. "Well. Damn. I wasn't expecting that."

I shrugged. "I wasn't expecting to find my gorgeous perfect dream girl last Saturday night, but here we are."

She smiled warmly. "Best of luck, sir," she said, turning on her heel and leaving quickly.

Glancing at the list, I turned to my computer and instantly searched the Renaissance Pub. It was in a quieter neighborhood, and seemed to be a low-key local bar.

Their social media pages had lots of photos of nice, normal people enjoying a drink after work. There were photos of big birthday parties, and smiling bartenders waving cocktail shakers. In one photo, a bartender was pouring a bright blue drink for two young ladies at the bar.

One of them was my Eden.

**9**

---

EDEN

** Language **

By Thursday, I would have thought that I could put Eric out of my mind for more than ten seconds. But it was impossible.

After finishing my classes for the day, I tried to get ahead of some of my reading but couldn't focus. I heard my phone beep, and almost burst into tears. I couldn't believe that Eric hadn't given up by now. Having a man that wonderful, who obviously liked me, was an incredible gift.

Yet I could not take the chance that something bad would happen to either of us. I could never live with myself if Eric was suddenly hit by a car because of the curse. If something happened to him and not me, I would be devastated. Naturally, I didn't want to be injured either. It just wasn't a chance that I could logically take.

Then my phone beeped three times in quick succession.

Kelly always sent rapid-fire messages. I ignored Eric's texts for fear of being heartbroken yet again, and went directly to Kelly's. She demanded that I meet her at Renaissance Pub, our usual local hangout. Apparently, she had a rough day, plus she hadn't had a chance to tell me all about the bearded man from Saturday night.

Looking around my tiny apartment, I could either stay here and wallow in self-pity for the evening, or go catch up with my friend. Before I'd even thought it through completely, I responded to her text, telling her I would be there at seven.

I brushed my hair, threw on minimal makeup, and found a comfortable but flattering gray patterned dress. It sort of looked like clouds, which made me think of the dark cloud hanging over me. It might have been a bit emo, but it was how I was feeling at the moment.

I walked to the pub, strolling in to see Kelly sitting in a large booth.

"Jamie just left," she said. "I was hoping that you could meet him, but it's his brother's birthday so he had to get to dinner."

"I take it that Jamie is your sexy bearded guy from last weekend?"

"Yes," she said, her eyes absolutely sparkling. She went on to tell me some of the sordid details, including the fact that he still had a waterbed, and was incredibly skilled with his hands.

Strangely, I found myself blushing less than usual during her raunchy tale.

"I don't know how official we are yet," she said, "But we're going out again Saturday night, so that's something."

Our regular bartender Todd was working tonight, so Kelly only had to wave to order us two Blue Beaches.

The second they arrived, we both took a sip, then she turned to lean in closer. "Now you must tell me every detail of what happened with that hunk you were dancing with. Did I actually see you kissing him?"

This time the blush shot through me from my eyebrows to my hips. Kelly's mouth fell open. I didn't even realize her eyes could get that wide. "Holy fucking shit. You went home with him."

"Wait, wait," I said, holding up my hands. "It was really late, and I was tipsy. So he took me home to crash at his place."

Kelly was literally on the edge of her seat, practically twitching. "And?"

I honestly wasn't sure how much I could share. It felt private. It felt like a secret I wanted to keep to myself. "He has a very nice condo," I said slowly.

"And? You had better tell me everything."

"Well, he was a perfect gentleman. I woke up in the morning with my clothes on, and a wall of pillows between us because he thought he would reach for me in the night and snuggle me in his sleep."

Kelly made a little puppy dog whimper. "Oh my God, that's so dorky and so adorable at the same time."

"Yeah, he was amazing, but–"

"Psst." Kelly nodded to the door. "Isn't that him?"

I glanced up to see Eric turning toward me. As soon as he recognized me, his eyes widened. Was he surprised?

"Sherbert."

Kelly laughed. "Watch your language."

There was no way that Eric could be here. I'd certainly never seen him here before. Having him appear out of the blue felt a bit creepy. Did he know I'd be here? Yet this was a public place.

Eric walked slowly toward us, and I felt myself biting my lip.

I took a quick sip of my drink then set it down, trying to arrange my hands casually in my lap, but nothing felt right. I didn't think he'd make a scene, but I really didn't know him that well.

He came over slowly, sitting beside me on the bench, picking up my hands. "If I did anything to hurt you or offend you in any way, I'm so sorry, Eden."

"I... um. No, that's not it."

His deep sigh of relief washed his warm breath over our clasped hands. "Thank god," he muttered. Then he looked over to Kelly. "Hello," he said politely, extending one hand. "I'm Eric."

"Kelly," she said, shaking his hand while looking completely confused.

She slid over to make more room for him on the bench. I automatically moved over as well, and he slid over to sit close beside me, holding both of my hands again.

"Eden," he said softly. Then he just stared into my eyes, his thumbs caressing my skin. It was as if we were the only two people in the world.

Kelly got up and went to the bar, muttering, "I'll just give you two a minute."

Under any other circumstances, I would have grabbed her hand and told her not to leave me with a strange man. But Eric wasn't a stranger. He was odd. He was completely fixated on me. He made my stomach feel pink and sparkly. He was definitely the one Nana warned me about. And he just appeared out of nowhere.

"Please," he said softly. "If there's another man, break my heart now. Make it clean. It would be a mercy killing."

I shook my head quickly, my hair falling slightly into my face. "No," I whispered. "There's nobody else."

He raised one hand, tucking back my hair, trailing his fingertips behind my ear. Then slowly down my neck. I had to press my lips together to hold back a whimper. He was so gorgeous that my eyes didn't know quite where to settle on his face. But those eyes were like magnets, drawing me back again and again.

"Are you leaving the country?" he said gently. "You have an internship in Italy, and you don't want to start something just before you leave?"

I tried to smile. "I'm so sorry, Eric, I just can't."

He finally took his fingers from my neck, holding his thumb near his lips. "She knows that if she doesn't give me some reason that it's going to eat away at me forever." Looking at his hand, he nodded. "I'm sure she knows that. I'm not sure if she knows that she's the sweetest, most beautiful, most fascinating woman I've ever met."

Giggles bubbled out of me uncontrollably.

"Maybe she's scared," he continued, nodding. "Maybe she knows that I'm positively head over heels for her, and it's a bit overwhelming." He held his thumb higher as if to listen, then nodded. "Okay, I'll ask."

Cocking his head, his eyes locked with mine and I felt like I was falling. "I know we slept together really fast, but that's not normal for me either. Eden, couldn't we just go on a few innocent dates? That way you'll get to know me, and know that I'm a very nice guy." His grin flashed a bit of his perfect teeth. "I have references."

My body was pulling forward. I needed to kiss him so badly that my lips were parting. My head was beginning to tilt. I couldn't let this happen. He was so sweet to me, and it felt like he'd be so good for me in every way. If I kissed him one more time it would all be over. There must be a way to–

"Two reasons," I squeaked, quickly leaning back just a heartbeat before he kissed me.

His eyes tightened, but he nodded. "Okay. Tell me."

"Crumpets," I muttered, looking down at his shoulder. I just couldn't meet his eyes.

"You can't date me because of odd British breakfast food?" His chuckle was forced. It was still adorable.

"That's just my non-cursing," I nearly whispered.

His hand darted out to run his thumb along my cheekbone, making me shiver. "I've heard you curse," he said softly. "It was the sexiest, most incredible time of my life."

I tried to lean back further, and he brought his hand back to hold mine again. "I'll behave. Tell me." His tone was very slightly demanding, and I hated how arousing that was.

I closed my eyes. I couldn't confess this while he was looking at me. "I gave a man my heart," I breathed, feeling him lean in to hear me. "He... hurt me so badly. I can't–"

"Oh, Eden, I'm so sorry," he said gently. "If it's too soon, I'll wait."

I could feel myself trembling, but felt I needed to spit out the other part.

"And..." My throat started to close as I felt the tears coming. It was too insane, but maybe he had a right to know. I didn't want to hurt him, but he was right. Better to make a clean break. He gave my hands a tiny shake of encouragement.

"My Nana sometimes blurts out strange sayings. Sort of like a prophecy or a curse," I said. "Everything she's ever said in her whispery tone has come true. Anyone who doesn't heed her warnings ends up hurt in some way."

"Okay," he said. "What does that have to do with me?"

I swallowed hard. "She warned me about you specifically." Jumping up, I grabbed my purse and slid out the far side of the bench, looking for Kelly. "I have to go."

Racing for the door, he caught me on the sidewalk, grabbing my wrist, but releasing me instantly. "Please," he begged. "You have to tell me what she said."

Looking up at him through a blur of tears, I whispered, "She said, 'Never get in bed with the devil. He lives for darkness and fire'."

Kelly appeared in the nick of time, and I grabbed her hand, walking quickly away. She slipped an arm around me, not even asking, knowing that I'd tell her in a while.

Somehow my head turned back to stare at him for another blurry blink. It was the worst thing I could have done.

Eric nearly collapsed against the wall, his eyes filled with such a stunned, horrified expression that I began to really cry. Turning back, Kelly got me into a cab and home, where I could vent the horrors of my ruined potentially perfect relationship.

# 10

ERIC

* Superstitions *

I knew there was no way I could simply tell Eden not to listen to her grandmother. Even though I knew that people didn't just spew out prophecies, and that superstitious thinking was illogical, I couldn't ignore her feelings. It was hard to dismiss some of the illogical things we believed.

She hadn't said why she thought her grandmother's declarations were absolute, so I couldn't try to figure out her line of thinking.

The only thing I knew with absolute certainty was that we belonged together. Admitting that to myself was down-right weird.

I knew that somewhere down the road I would want to settle down, get married, and have kids. I wanted a house outside of the city. I wanted a family. A lot of people wanted that just because it's what we had been trained to desire. But I knew in my heart it's what I truly craved.

I didn't want any girl who would be a good mother. I wanted someone who would laugh with me. Someone who would smack my ass when I was in her way in the kitchen. I needed someone with sass, who wasn't afraid to throw it back at me.

I needed a sweet, pretty girl who never said a bad word unless she was in the throes of passion.

I needed Eden.

It wasn't just the nearly insane level of lust I felt for her. I adored her voice. I liked the way she looked at things as if she were analyzing them. I liked that she seemed a bit particular and fussy about a few things. She had a mind of her own. She wasn't trying to please me with every step.

To process all of this, I knew I was going to have to do something serious. Something that was probably unexpected, but she had to know that it would be coming someday. I'm sure Eden knew on some level that there was no way I could just let her go.

Friday evening, I called my sister and invited her over. Angie seemed a bit surprised, and arrived right away.

We always had a great relationship in life and business, but emotionally we had sort of been at arm's length most of our lives.

Angie was only a year and a half younger than I, so we fought like cats and dogs through our teenage years. But once we hit our twenties and realized after university that we had the same goals, we'd become a solid team.

My sister was a financial wizard, and I trusted her completely. Building a company with her wasn't exactly easy, but it was steady. She always had my back. Plus, she had the added bonus of stealth.

It was disgusting that a lot of men in the business and

construction worlds assumed that the woman in the black suit dress was some sort of assistant or intern. She heard everything, then used it to her advantage.

Watching men expect her to fetch coffee, then have her stand up to lead the meeting was brilliant. They were completely disarmed, and it usually dropped their poker faces.

Angie used it to her advantage every chance she got, and I often helped her. It was their own fault if they made any assumptions about her. It was often all I could do to stop from laughing in their faces.

As soon as Angie arrived, I led her to the couch. "Whiskey or tea?" I asked.

She flashed her usual smirk. Angie looked a bit plain from afar, with her dark hair skimmed back into a tight ponytail, and her classic but understated features. Then her eyes blazed, and she looked absolutely ferocious.

"I don't know what kind of conversation this is, so you pick."

Fussing around for a moment, I set two glasses with ice in front of us, and poured a generous shot and a half of smooth rye.

Holding up her glass, she said, "To us making sense of whatever has you so freaked out."

I nodded, as we drank. Setting down the glass, I got straight to the point. "I accidentally met the girl of my dreams. Her grandmother apparently says prophetic things, and warned her against getting into bed with the devil. She found out what my real name means, and now she's avoiding me."

Angie looked at me flatly. Then she picked up her glass, took a big swallow, and set it down. "Jesus Christ," she muttered. "The things you get yourself into."

"Yes, I'm a walking disaster," I said, rolling my eyes. "Problem solving mode, please. How do I prove to her that she should date me for a while?"

Angie made a giggling snort noise. "Date? I thought people just hooked up these days."

I decided right then to never tell my sister how Eden and I met. "Honestly, sis, she's the one. I'd bet the company on it."

She froze and looked at me wide-eyed. We only ever used that expression when we were drop dead serious. "Shit. Okay." She stared into space for a moment. "You changed your name a little. Does that count?"

I shook my head. "Apparently not."

Angie uncrossed her legs and sat up straighter. It was her stance for thinking on the spot during meetings, and I appreciated that she was going into business mode for me.

"Do these prophecies wear off over time?" she asked. "If it was said over a year ago, does it still count?"

"Good thinking," I said, pulling out my phone and making a quick note.

"Is there a way to break the curse, or whatever?" she asked. "I don't know anything about those New Age rituals, but people wave burning sage around to get rid of bad vibes or something. Maybe you could wear a crystal, or dance naked under the full moon or whatever?"

I shook my head. "I don't think she's the New Age type. She seems quite logical. Sharp."

Angie nodded. "Okay. Logic."

She stared at a spot on the coffee table very intently. Then she inhaled sharply, snapping her fingers. "The words she used were, 'don't get into bed with the devil', right?"

"Yes."

Angie grinned. "So don't go to bed with her. Just date her

until she falls completely in love with you. And you know," her eyes narrowed, "If you're going to get busy, do it in the back of a car, or on a couch or something. Not in a bed."

I nodded, laughing. "This is why I keep you around, sis." She had always been the best at finding loopholes in contracts, and missing clarification.

Angie shrugged. "This might sound completely strange, but there's another thing you could do."

"Anything."

"You could go ask the grandmother what the hell she was talking about. I mean, for all you know, she could have meant something completely different. She could have been specifically referencing men named Lucifer. Or people from hot places. Who knows? The key to a successful contract is excessive detail. Maybe the same works with a prophecy?"

"Well, damn. How could I not have thought of that?"

Angie grinned. "Men think of breaking down walls. Women think of building bridges to go over them."

"Yeah, yeah. Creators and destroyers." We'd had similar versions of this conversation over the years.

"Well, stop trying to break the curse. Find ways around it, through it. Work with her. If she's so amazing, and you think she's into you, be on her team." Something in Angie's usually controlled expression flickered. "Also, find out if she's had her heart broken. That can change everything."

"Shit. She did mention that."

"Then be on her team, no matter what the outcome," Angie said gently. "Even if you end up just a pleasant diversion to help her heal."

I nodded. "Yeah. I want Eden to be happy, above all else."

"Her name is Eden?"

"Yeah."

Angie burst out laughing. "The devil in the garden. Damn, that's hilarious."

I didn't find it as funny as she did, but it was pretty bizarre.

# 11

---

## EDEN



At the time when Andy and I broke up, I didn't think that my heartache could possibly be any worse, at any point in my life.

So this new level of angst completely blindsided me. I'd always taken my time, getting to know someone before finding out whether or not we clicked physically. Now that I'd had a little time and space, I could honestly say that Andy and I never really clicked physically. He didn't send sparks shooting through me from a simple touch on my arm. His kisses didn't make me weak in the knees.

Not like Eric. The indescribable desire to be near him was like a hot shimmering halo around me at all times. I honestly felt changed from one strange night and morning together.

I didn't know whether to be horrified that he discovered what pub I hung out at, or impressed. My gut reaction was that I was touched he would go to so much trouble. But it was also a little extreme.

Yet having to look into his eyes while I hurt him was too much to bear. I'd never had a very healthy level of self-esteem, and it had taken a major hit when I'd been dumped so hard. Trying to see myself in a new light, through Eric's sweet gaze, was oddly thrilling.

It was absolutely impossible to concentrate on writing my essay, and choosing classes for next term. Every single thing about the field of writing and English had always excited me, but now everything seemed dull and slightly blurry.

I wanted to ask Eric his opinion on what classes I should take. I wanted to ask him what he thought about language changing in each form of media, to help me get my next essay started.

I wanted to ask if he would ever forgive me for making him feel... Whatever he was feeling when I saw that horrific expression on his face as I walked away.

Rubbing my eyes roughly to try to stop the tears, I told myself that telling him the truth was better than beating around the bush and trying to let him down easy. Some things were just out of our control, and this was one of those situations.

I just wished that I could see straight, and that this hole where a heart should be would stop throbbing with phantom pain.

I couldn't take a chance by going against The Knowing. It would be one thing if I was hurt, but if Eric was with me when something terrible happened, I would never forgive myself.

Venting everything with Kelly over a bottle of cheap wine was helpful. She'd heard the stories of my weird family over the years, and she agreed that a declaration from Nana was not something that could be messed with.

She was very happy that I'd clicked with someone though. It gave her another opportunity to rant about how horrible Andy was, and how I'd find someone soon who treated me well. Kelly was an excellent cheerleader, but once she left, I'd sunk into a pit of despair again.

Two days later, I was still unable to concentrate properly. There was no way in heck I was going to let myself become one of those girls who messed up their grades because of some guy.

I was almost relieved when my phone rang with an unknown number. If it was a stupid sales call, at least it would be a distraction for a moment.

"Hello?" I said, hearing my voice hitch.

"Eden, it's Eric. Please don't hang up. Please just listen for two minutes."

My throat closed as I burst into tears again. I didn't know whether I should be angry that he was using another number. It was a bit shifty. But it was such a relief to hear his voice that I wanted to forgive it.

"Oh God, baby... Don't cry. Please. Just listen, okay?"

"Okay," I barely managed to squeak.

"Your Nana said don't go to bed with the devil, right?"

He was speaking very quickly as if he needed to spit it all out before I hung up. But I knew I had to hear him out. "The only time we were in bed, we were just sleeping. And we weren't really together, there was a wall of pillows between us, remember? Also, you didn't get into bed with me. I put you to bed. I know that sounds like a very minuscule difference, but in a court of law, it would hold up. Don't you think?"

"Maybe?"

"Okay, stay with me. We had sex in the kitchen. That's

not in bed. In the shower, which is not in bed. So I think it's reasonably safe to say that we haven't crossed the curse yet. Are you with me so far?"

"Yes. I guess so."

"So I don't feel like it would be breaking any rules if you and I sat down over a coffee and had a business meeting about the situation."

I was so distraught that a giggle burst out of me like a hiccup. "Business meeting?"

"Yes. We could meet in a coffee shop, and just have a chat." He paused, and I heard his voice soften. "Partly because I really need to know that you're alright. It's killing me to hear you so upset."

He stayed silent for a moment, allowing me to take a breath. "It hurts," I choked. "I miss you. And I feel like maybe seeing you again will make everything hurt even more."

I heard him sigh. "You know I don't want that."

"I know."

"I miss you so much," he murmured. It felt like he was practically nuzzling my ear. "How about we have coffee, and a calm chat, and we will figure out a way to either get past this, or stay friendly acquaintances. Does that sound reasonable?"

I nodded, then almost laughed when I realized he couldn't see it. "Yes. Okay."

Eric sounded completely relieved. "How about Mowat's Cafe near King and Yonge? Tomorrow at six? They're usually slow that time of day. I go there sometimes to do a little extra paperwork and get out of my office."

"All right. I'll see you then," I said.

"Eden," he said gently, "I appreciate you taking a chance

on this. On us. I don't know what you've been through, but it sounds like it's been really hard. I don't want to make anything worse for you. I think you're being very brave."

"Thank you," I squeaked, but I ended the call quickly as the tears took over again.

I was fully aware that meeting up with him might be the craziest thing I'd ever done. I didn't like the thought of following the letter, and not the spirit of the law. It felt shifty. But he was right that technically we hadn't gone against Nana's prophecy. Or, warning. Whatever The Knowing was.

My family had never discussed it in great detail. If I was going to consider not being with this amazing guy out of fear of a strange power, I should know more about it.

Although I had always been much closer to my grandmother than my mother, I didn't feel right about asking Nana directly. So I called my Mom.

"Hi, sweetie," she trilled. "I haven't heard from you in ages. How are you?"

"I'm pretty good, keeping busy."

We caught up on our daily lives for a few minutes, but I knew that she could tell I had a point to get to. "So, what's up?" she asked.

"Okay, so you know when Nana sort of zones out, and says something to the ceiling? You know how what she says then always comes true?"

"We are not discussing this," Mom said sharply. "What else is new with you?"

"Come on. This is important."

I could almost hear my mother shaking her head as she always did when she was upset. "It's bad luck to talk about it," she said in a very strange, tight tone. "I can't."

"Relax," I said. "I just want to ask about the process, and what it is."

"No. Have a nice day, sweetie."
My mother actually hung up on me. Biscuits.

**12**

---

ERIC

** Dark Gray Suit **

I had pitched proposals for building construction worth over six hundred million dollars. I had negotiated deals with CEOs of the most gigantic tech corporations. I'd negotiated with politicians, city planners, and all sorts of anal-retentive bureaucratic people.

At no point in my life had I ever prepared for a meeting with this level of overzealous precision, even though I had barely any information to work with. My coffee chat with Eden would be my most important meeting ever.

I consulted with Patricia to help me pick a suit and tie that would make me look the most non-threatening and appealing. She told me to go with the darkest gray since it was softer than black. She remembered that I had a caramel and peach swirl tie that was softer than most of my plain bold colors.

Calling my sister, I asked Angie if bringing flowers would be too much. She agreed that it would. She assured me that any gifts at this point might be taken the wrong way.

Skimming the news, I made note of all light, entertaining topics, in case she brought something up. I checked the weather.

I reviewed everything I knew about Eden, and tried to think of any way to disprove her belief in her grandmother's so-called powers without insulting her in any way. I couldn't tell her it was silly to believe in something. It was obviously a family tradition, of sorts.

I looked up a bunch of facts on premonitions, psychic ability, and prophecies. The proven rate of accuracy was almost zero. The few instances where accurate things were foretold, they were so vague that it was easily a coincidence. I didn't want to spring all of this on her, but I had a bunch of notes loaded in my phone in case the topic came up.

Getting to the coffee shop early, I spoke with the owner, explaining the situation as briefly as possible. Since I was a regular, he agreed to keep the music in the back room soft and upbeat, while encouraging all customers to sit in the front so that we had a bit of privacy.

Nervousness was not an emotion I ever allowed to come to the forefront. It only happened if you were not prepared enough, I had always told myself before presentations.

If you were nervous, that meant there was potential for failure. Acknowledging that potential was no way to walk into a meeting. It was better to walk in already knowing the outcome. Believing it. Knowing it in your heart through and through.

As I sat in the back of the café, frantically drumming my fingers on the table, I was struck by my realization that I was superstitious as well. I had my own patterns of belief that were completely illogical. But I believed them because it worked for me.

Holy shit.

There was no way that I should try to talk Eden out of believing in her grandmother's words. I should help her find a way around instead.

**13**

---

EDEN

** Just Business **

I actually had to call in a favor to have someone proofread an assignment that was due. My eyes were slightly blurry with tears that wouldn't stop.

Having always been a person that played by the rules, sticking to things that were logically the next step, I was torn into pieces from trying to figure out what to do about Eric. It should be a yes or no decision. Because of Nana's whispers, it should be no.

Yet he made me feel more complete, and more cherished than anyone I'd ever been with before.

Once I corrected the seventeen typos that my friend caught for me, I emailed my assignment off. Splashing cold water on my face, I started to get ready. A lot of makeup would be a mistake, so I smudged on a little waterproof eyeliner, and tried to look awake with a bit of blush.

Although I wanted to stay in my slouchy track pants and worn-out sweater, that didn't put me in the mindset of a business meeting. It was rather adorable that Eric wanted to frame it this way, to help me stay calm. I found a long, dark purple dress that looked quite nice, but was as comfortable as a nightgown.

Picking up Eric's hoodie from my dresser, I couldn't resist burying my nose in it. It smelled very faintly of his lemon soap. Rolling it up, I stuffed it in my huge purse, resolving to give it back to him.

As I walked to the café, I tried to figure out how open I should be with him. If we were ending things before they even started, there was no sense in telling him how big my feelings already were. I'd have to hold it together.

I wanted to stand outside of my mind and give myself a good talking to. Like yelling at a movie when the girl at home alone goes down to the basement to investigate a scary noise. We should know better. I should know better. But I was going anyway.

Even though I arrived five minutes early, Eric was at a table in the back, with a coffee already prepared for me. He had also set a glass of water and a muffin in front of the empty chair beside him.

As soon as I approached, he stood up, holding out his arms tentatively. "May I hug you?"

I tumbled into his arms, trying desperately not to cry, but he could sense it. "Shh, baby, please." I heard his voice hitch as if he were overcome with emotion as well. "You get it all out," he said as he stroked my back gently. "But it's killing me that you're upset."

Nodding against his chest, I tried to inhale his warmth. His strength. After a moment, I took another deep breath, then straightened up, sitting down and trying to focus. He sat down beside me and took a sip of coffee.

"What did you want to talk about?" I said in a tiny voice.

"You mentioned that there were two reasons why we couldn't be together," he said gently. "I don't want to upset you, and I don't want you to share more than you're comfortable with. But I thought that perhaps if you were to tell me a bit about both, we could try to see if these are hurdles that we could overcome."

I nodded, taking a sip of coffee while I tried to steady myself. Something about the rich, earthy fragrance always made me feel more grounded.

"I guess I'll start with the one that's easier to explain," I said slowly. "Six months ago, I broke up with a guy. Andy and I had only dated for around six months, but it was like..." I stared down at my hands, fussing with my thumbnail.

"I guess I wanted that part of my life to be a checkmark instead of an empty space," I said, trying to explain it to myself as much as to Eric. "It was so hard to learn how to speak with guys, and open myself up. I didn't want to think I'd ever have to do that again."

I realized that sounded pathetic. Wow.

"Holy squid," I muttered more to myself than to Eric, "I'm so nervous about relationships that I'd rather stay in a lousy one than try again." I looked up at him in shock.

Instead of acknowledging that I'm an idiot, he looked disturbed. "Eden, I didn't realize that it was so hard for you. No wonder I freaked you out, coming on so strong, so fast."

"You know, Andy looked good on paper," I said lamely. "He had finished university, had a great job. He came from a nice family."

"How did he treat you?" Eric asked quietly.

My automatic shrug probably spoke volumes. "He was nice to me when he wanted something, like for me to show up in a quirky dress, playing the part of his cute girlfriend when his coworkers had a party." I paused. "We spent more time at his work social events then alone, to be honest. He was always telling me that I needed to drop ten pounds and get my hair cut so that I'd show up better in the photos."

I heard a slight clicking noise, and looked over to see that it was Eric's jaw clenching, vibrating.

"Andy... What did you say his last name was?"

"Marsh, but it doesn't matter."

I watched as Eric made a quick note on his phone. I couldn't help smirking. "Don't bother going after him. He's not worth it."

He reached over to give my hand a little squeeze. "Your curves are part of your... Awesomosity? Is that a word? Whatever. I think you are ravishing, and anyone who suggests you should change who you are deserves a swift, hard slap." He shot me a grin. "Please continue."

I exhaled hard, then blurted out the shortest version of the story of Andy planning to dump me while my mother was in the hospital. And how he had been using me the entire time.

The clicking got louder.

"Well, I'm glad that you got to be the one to do the dumping, in a way," Eric said. "I cannot fucking stand that he made you feel small. That he used you."

This time I wasn't sure what my shrug was saying. "That's what normal girls have to deal with, I guess," I said quietly. "We get what we get and we hope for the best."

"No." He practically spat the word at me. "Eden, you are extraordinary. You are funny and light. You are gorgeous. You are ridiculously sweet, and have a halo of warmth around you that colors everything you do and say."

Nobody had ever said anything like that to me before,

and my mouth actually fell open for a second. "I... I don't..." I sputtered.

"Andy Marsh is human-shaped garbage," Eric said with a touch of darkness in his voice. "If you ever want to see me as the devil, you put him in front of me for ten seconds. I will give that fucker the punishment he deserves."

Seeing how riled up Eric was just thinking of the man who had hurt me warmed my heart in a way I couldn't understand. I could see that Eric would always defend me. Protect me. I would be completely safe around him if it wasn't for... the curse.

"So, I see that it might take you a little time and space to work through the nastiness that was your ex-boyfriend. If that's an issue, we can take our relationship incredibly slowly if you like."

Then he paused. "Would you like to try to explain this curse from your grandmother now? What exactly do you mean? Is she psychic?"

"I don't know, exactly." I stared down at my hands while they twitched slightly. "I don't think I really believe in psychic powers. In fact, I'm pretty sure that I don't."

"Well, I don't," Eric said, "But I will be extremely open-minded while you try to explain what this thing is."

I nodded, taking another sip of coffee. I tried to let the quiet energy of the café wash over me, calming me so I could think this through.

"Nana doesn't announce that she's making a declaration or anything. She sort of zones out, and whispers to the ceiling. Or occasionally down at her teacup. We jot down whatever she said, then it usually comes true or makes sense in a couple of days, or weeks."

"Does every single thing come true?"

"We've never exactly kept score," I said. "But lots of them do."

"Okay. Could you tell me some examples?"

I reached out to squeeze his knee, smiling over to him. "I really appreciate that you're listening, and not just telling me I'm nuts."

Eric flashed me an adorable wink. "I only think you're a bit nuts in a good way. Go on."

I nodded, thinking. "There was one time Nana said something like, 'No blue cars on the highway today'."

He nodded. "That does sound ominous."

"Yeah. About a week later my Uncle Nick had to rent a car, and had his choice of blue or silver. He had to drive on the highway, so he picked the silver one. When he returned the car, the sales guy said he made a good choice, because the blue one's engine cut out while it was being driven. He could have been in an accident."

Eric nodded. "Okay. More likely he would have been stranded on the highway. Not quite life and death, but strangely precise. Tell me another."

"My Mom mentioned a former coworker who had won a few hundred dollars in the lottery. A few minutes later, Nana whispered something about, 'You'll never win the game if you don't really play'."

He chuckled. "That's just good advice. You can't dream of winning if you don't buy a ticket once in a while."

"Yes – that's exactly what my mother thought. So she went out that day to buy a ticket and won a thousand dollars."

Eric pursed his lips, drumming his fingers on the table-top. "That could be considered good luck, not really a curse or a prophecy."

"Okay. There was one time Nana whispered, 'Stay ahead

of the curve, because the darkness is coming.' My sister Eva was doing a paper on some programming curve thing. She's really into software tech, I didn't understand it. Because of Nana's whispers, she raced to finish her paper before the power went out in a storm that night."

I glanced at Eric. "She would have failed if she didn't get that assignment in on time, and the wifi doesn't work when the power is out."

Eric turned, taking both of my hands in his. "Are you afraid that if you date someone who could technically be thought of as the devil, that something bad will happen to me?"

I nodded seriously, squeezing his hands.

"I don't want to go through life with you thinking there is some shadow of dread hanging over us," he said. "I don't want you to be scared of what we have."

His deep eyes locked onto mine. "You feel this, don't you, Eden? This isn't a fling. We're good for each other. We're right for each other."

I swallowed hard so my throat wouldn't close. I knew he was right, and I wasn't sure why I was becoming tearful again. "I was so sure during the last relationship, even though all evidence pointed to it being a disaster. Now that everything looks incredible, absolutely too good to be true, I don't know what I would do if this fell apart." I had to tear my eyes away from his. "It's all too much."

Eric slipped his arm around me, sliding his chair closer so I could lean into his shoulder. "I know I'm supposed to be the big strong man here, with all of the answers, but I'm going to tell you a secret." He turned to the coffee cup. "Should I tell her? Will she think I'm being a wuss?" He nodded. "Okay."

I laughed, shaking against him.

"Eden," he said, stroking my hair gently, "I'm scared too. I've never dated anyone for more than a few weeks, maybe a month or two. I've never had feelings anywhere close to what I feel for you. This is all brand new territory. Uncharted waters."

He rocked me gently, making me feel safe and warm, as if we were the only two people in the world. "Baby, what if we just dated for a while? No getting into bed. Even though these gigantic feelings I have for you are very serious, perhaps we could just stick to the light side for a while. You could come over for a movie. I can go to your place and make you dinner. Little dates, and normal conversations."

I nodded. "That sounds extremely logical."

His thick arms tightened around me. "Of course we have to be logical. This is a very important business meeting. Our relationship is the most important project I have on my plate right now."

Giggling, I said, "I would love to see you in a board meeting. Honestly, I can't imagine you being serious for twenty straight minutes. Do you start talking to inanimate objects when there are grownups around?"

He waggled his eyebrows. "Maybe you'll never know."

"Seriously, I can't even picture you in an office."

"It's only a few blocks away. Would you like to see it? The view from the fifty-first floor is pretty spectacular."

"Wow." I sat up straight and drank the last sip of my coffee. "Sure, a walk together would be nice."

Eric grinned, looking extremely relieved.

As we stood up and I grabbed my purse, I asked, "Were the results of this meeting satisfactory?"

He tucked my hair back behind both ears, holding the sides of my face as he gently kissed my forehead. "Absolutely. We are still in negotiations. Everything is still on the table. We are switching locations and having a field trip to check out a new site. These are all excellent things."

He took my hand as we walked out of the café. "Plus, the elevator is really fast. I'm secretly hoping that you'll get a bit frightened and grab me inappropriately."

I giggled like crazy, secretly hoping that he wasn't kidding.

**14**

---

ERIC

** Building **

I was relieved when Eden allowed me to hold her hand while we walked. We strolled slowly, looking in shop windows, and chatting about our favorite restaurants. We had a surprising amount of things in common, from our love of indie rock music to our mutual lust of authentic Mexican food.

When we turned toward the office tower where my business took up an entire floor, Eden stopped walking to lean her head back, staring up at the blue-tinted glass. "Which one is your office?" she laughed.

"It's on the other side," I grinned, leading her inside.

I was used to zipping through the lobby in a hurry, but this time I tried to walk slowly and see it through her eyes. All of the marble and glass, with gigantic expensive sculptures, must be rather impressive if you're not used to it.

The security guard jumped up, giving me an almost military nod. "Good evening, Mr. Stone."

"Hey, Gary. Quiet tonight?"

"I certainly hope so."

"Excellent," I nodded. Guiding us into an open elevator, I swiped my card and hit the button for fifty-one.

Sure enough, once we picked up speed, Eden squealed and buried her face in my chest. "Holy squid, how do you get used to this!"

"It's not that fast," I chuckled.

"Maybe I'm just used to buildings with slow elevators," she said. "This feels super high tech."

"This building is only six years old, so you're probably right."

The doors slid open and I led her through the silent lobby. Since it was a quarter after seven, the entire office was abandoned. Angie and I had spread the word that we would prefer people not work late unless there was something truly crucial going on. We knew that some companies rewarded their workers for putting in excruciating hours. We would rather reward people for being efficient. People were sharper when they had sufficient rest and relaxation.

I looked over to see Eden's expression, and she was absolutely grinning at the huge Two Stones logo on the wall over the long, sleek reception desk.

"Yeah," I shrugged, "It's a bit ostentatious, but since we're in construction and building design, our clients expect a bit of a show."

Leading her down a long hallway, we passed an all-white office, and she stopped. The door was open, so she leaned in to see that one wall was painted bright teal, but the rest of the office had white walls, a white desk, white chair, and white shelf with white baskets to contain books and office supplies. The white shade was drawn, so there wasn't even a view of the city.

"Is this a punishment room?" she asked.

I must have laughed harder than she expected, as she seemed confused. "Instead of a huge office, my sister Angie wanted two small offices. There's a normal one for taking phone calls, having small meetings, and having her morning coffee. This is her focus room. When that door is shut, she might as well be on Mars. No one will disturb her."

Eden grinned. "Not even you?"

I shook my head quite seriously. "I would only knock on that door if the building were on fire. If there was something incredibly important, I would text her, and she would get back to me whenever she checked her phone."

"Wow." She seemed impressed. "I'd love to talk to Angie sometime about her focus techniques. It would probably help me with my schoolwork."

Pulling her close, I kissed the top of her hair. "I would love to have the two of you over for dinner. I know you two would click." Turning to a huge green abstract painting on the hallway wall, I said, "Yes, I know. The two of them would gang up on me and mock me mercilessly. It's a chance I'm willing to take for the most precious women in my life."

Ignoring Eden's giggles, we walked down to what used to be a medium-sized meeting room. Now there was a long table in front of the longest wall, covered in wooden buildings. "Cheese and crackers," she muttered, quickly walking over to look more closely.

I loved how excited she was. Eden was never trying to be cool, or act any particular way. She was authentic. Enthusiastic. She let her emotions bubble straight out of her, and I found that admirable.

We stared at the miniature Toronto set up for a while, and it was adorable watching her eyes track along the streets.

"When an architecture firm designs a building," I

explained, "They can sculpt or 3-D print a mock-up, and we can place it on the site. Then we can take photos of it from different angles. Sometimes they bring in a background, or a lighting system. Some people don't visualize very well, so it's best to show them before they spend millions upon millions constructing a building."

She looked up at me strangely, then shook her head. "I couldn't imagine having that much responsibility," she said.

"You will," I said. "Someday you'll be writing something that changes people's opinions. Or gives them information that they really need."

She rolled those pretty warm brown eyes at me dramatically. "Somehow I don't think it's the same thing."

"Who knows," I said. "You might end up writing brochures with us someday."

She shook her head quickly. "No, I'd never want you to hire me." Eden looked up at me, placing a hand in the center of my chest. "Sorry, I didn't mean for that to sound rude I just... After Andy wanted to use me to further his career, I'm grossed out by the concept of using inside connections."

I nodded, taking her hand to lead her down to the end of the hallway. "I get that. And I honestly cannot stand that some worm of a douche bag made you feel shitty."

Giving her a sideways glance as we reached my office door, I added, "Pardon my language. Crappy." She grinned, her nose crinkling as I swiped my pass card and went into my office.

"Holy Mother of Bob," she muttered.

I watched her walk right up to the floor to ceiling windows, pressing her nose to the glass as she looked down at the city below. Watching her eyes dart around the buildings and streets, I loved watching her analyze things.

Coming up to stand behind her, I wrapped my arms

around her waist, placing my hands on her stomach. "Just for a second," I said softly in her ear, "Let's pretend we are King and Queen of the city. What would you want to do first?"

Turning her shoulders, Eden leaned back against me until our entire bodies were pressing together as she tipped her chin up. Kissing her felt as natural as breathing. The way her lips gently pressed to mine felt absolutely exhilarating.

She spun in my arms, wrapping her hands around my shoulders, as our kiss became more heated. It was wild how this girl made me melt completely.

**15**

---

EDEN

** The Office **

ood grief, the way he touched me. The way his mouth met mine so gently, but with such fire. The way he built me up, making me feel better about myself.

Pushing his suit jacket open, I ran my hands down his shirt, feeling his abs clench as I reached them. Then he pulled away, his hands around my waist, staring at me as if he were trying to see through my soul.

I'd always been shy when anyone looked at me, but under Eric's gaze, I felt comfortable. Cherished.

His saucy grin told me he was definitely thinking of something naughty. He released me just long enough to lock the office door, and toss his jacket over his guest chair. His gigantic desk had nothing on it but a laptop, a notebook, and a pen, and he quickly slid all of that into a drawer.

"Come here," he nearly growled.

I loved it when his voice became dark. I loved when he

became a tiny bit demanding. It felt like he wanted me so badly he couldn't control himself.

Walking over to him, I dropped my purse on the floor, unfastening the top button of my dress. He grabbed my hips, sitting me up on the desk, standing between my knees as my head fell back to look up at him.

"I know we just said that we are going to take it slow," he said, "I'll stop any time you want me to. But every single male in the corporate world has a not so secret fantasy of having sex on his desk."

My head fell back even farther as I laughed. It was darling that he was openly aware of being super dorky.

"You're probably not ready to have sex with me again, and that's totally fine, but could we at least make out here for a minute?" He grinned, raising an eyebrow. "Make a tiny bit of my dirty fantasy come true?"

Looking up at his gorgeous face, those luscious lips I was starting to know too well, I was filled with that prickling wave of lust. He's the only man who had ever made me feel this way. Completely in touch with my own libido. Grounded in my body. As I spread my legs wider, I realized that he might find out exactly how aroused I was if he glanced at my wet panties.

Gripping the front of his shirt, I pulled his lips to mine, then began unbuttoning. Eric's low groan thrilled me to the core, then he began unbuttoning my dress down to my waist.

He helped me pull his shirt off, then laid me back, reaching under to unfasten my bra. Shoving the fabric out of the way, his hands wandered over my breasts so softly as he leaned in to kiss me. He was so gentle, his tongue against mine, his thumb swirling around my nipple.

There was no way I could tell him to stop. My blood was

dancing through my veins. My skin felt electrified. Looking up into those deep eyes and seeing how much he wanted me, I desperately needed to please both of us.

Fumbling between us, I unfastened his belt, then slipped my hand into his pants. His rumbling moan took over both of our mouths. Running my hand lightly along his shaft, it took less than a minute for it to be standing at complete attention.

"Eden, every time I see you I cannot believe how hot you are. You're my fantasy girl even without the desk."

Eric sat me up so that I could pull my entire dress off, and my bra. Then he eased me back against the glossy wooden surface, kissing along my neck.

"You're so beautiful," he murmured. "I'm the luckiest man in the world."

"I can't..." I started, then his teeth scraped lightly across my nipple, making me gasp.

Instantly he froze. "You can't... Do this? Do you want me to stop?"

I shook my head, grinning as I pulled his lips back down to my breast. I almost laughed as I realized that was possibly the most aggressive thing I'd ever done while nearly naked in my life.

"No, don't stop. I can't believe the way you make me feel this sexy."

"You are ridiculously sexy," he said, kissing down my stomach to the edge of my panties. Hooking his thumbs in the sides, he slid them down slowly as I lifted my butt for him. Although I was sure nobody could see in the windows, I felt oddly exposed.

The way his hands ran up my inner thighs, such a gentle caress, made me fall back against the desk, trying to relax completely. Eric pulled his desk chair over, sitting down as he spread me wide, his breath light against my open pussy.

Then he gave me the sweetest, gentlest kiss, brushing his lips against my clit, then working lower. His fingers slid up my legs, finding my entrance and slowly slipping inside.

I could feel how slick I was already. My knees pressed against his shoulders, and I felt a shudder run through him as he felt how wet I was. His tongue wound in circles around my most delicate skin, as two fingers pulsed inside me.

Part of me couldn't believe this was happening. A much bigger part of me wanted to be Eric's dream girl.

My fingertips grazed his cheek, and I felt like I was melting under the intensity of his gaze. Those dark eyes felt like they were willing me to come on his tongue.

My hips began grinding, straining, as he increased his rhythm slowly. Every motion was so deliberate, so careful. My back began to arch, my head falling back as I squirmed across his desk.

A flash of realization hit me. He would be picturing this moment on his desk for years to come, while signing important contracts and doing critical research.

My release was coming closer and closer, until I could almost see it. Curling forward, I gripped Eric's hair, pulling his tongue against my clit harder. He absolutely grinned, flashing me a wink.

That pushed me over the edge completely as I tumbled into a full body muscle spasm of pure bliss. "Fuck, oh fuck yes," I whispered, panting from the waves of desire overtaking me.

From the look in his eyes, I didn't know who was more satisfied, Eric or me. The way he touched me so confidently made me desperate for more. A wave of adrenaline hit me, and I stood up carefully, grabbing him so that he stood up as well.

"What are you..."

"Pants off," I demanded. He laughed as he helped me strip him naked, then I pushed him back into his office chair. Dropping to my knees, I backed under the desk slightly.

"Don't tell me that you haven't had this fantasy as well," I giggled, pulling the chair toward me slightly, then running my hands along his thighs.

Gripping his shaft carefully, I leaned forward and got comfortable. Wow, even his dick was gorgeous. Placing the head of his thickness on my bottom lip, I looked up at him. "Isn't this what the hot president of the big important company deserves?" I said in a high pitched bimbo voice.

He grinned as my tongue darted out, lapping around the entire head. Then his eyes half-closed and he groaned as I pulled him deeper, sucking half of his length into my mouth.

"Holy fuck," he murmured. Gripping the base carefully with both hands, I stroked along his length with both my palms and my lips, experimenting to see how much pressure he liked. He seemed to prefer a light touch. He definitely enjoyed watching my eyes as he looked down. His blinking pattern became erratic, as his hips began to shift in the leather seat.

I never realized how powerful a blow job could be. I'd only done it twice before, and I was told that I was not very skilled. But every touch along Eric's smooth, hard flesh seemed to excite him more.

Feeling him thicken and throb in my hands was making my pussy quiver. I needed to be filled. I needed him to take me. But more than that, I needed to satisfy my man. I wanted him to remember this forever.

Very gently he placed his hand at the back of my head, and I nodded eagerly. Without pushing, he guided me to move more quickly.

His eyes became wider as he stared at me, seeming incredulous. Moving faster, I pressed my lips more firmly, trying to milk every ounce of sensation from him.

"Eden," he choked, "Where... Oh fuck. Where do you want..."

I hoped that he could see my grin in my eyes, since my lips were stretched tight around his girth. Trying to relax my throat and breathe through my nose, I moaned, pulling him deeper. As he realized I was telling him that I intended to swallow, his fingers clenched in the back of my hair.

"Oh, fuck, baby," he grunted, then I tasted his salty-sweet release across my tongue and down my throat. I moaned loudly, as he seemed to enjoy the vibrations. Swallowing quickly, I lapped up every drop, amused by the way he stared at me with his mouth hanging open.

"Wow," he muttered, leaning back in his chair.

Smiling sweetly, I got up to sit in his lap. He was looking at me with the level of intensity one would expect if you'd just run into your favorite movie star.

"What?" I giggled. "I've watched a few dirty videos."

"You're amazing," he murmured, gripping my ass as he pulled me against him. I loved that he kissed me hard, even knowing where my mouth had just been. There was something so primal and perfect about the two of us being naked where we weren't supposed to be.

**16**

---

ERIC

** Big Desk **

**M**y sweet, shy girl certainly got fired up easily. This strange connection of ours seemed to become more intoxicating every time we were together. Looking into her magical eyes as she grinned, I adored that she was obviously proud of herself. She should be. Seeing her so happy was extremely satisfying.

Feeling my cock begin to twitch again was a relief. Pulling her so that she was straddling me, her knees were on either side of my hips on the wide leather chair.

Leaning back slightly, I held her shoulders until her mouth settled over mine. She kissed me seductively, her hot ass grinding against me slightly. Then her eyes flew wide as she realized what was coming back to life.

"Really?" she smiled.

"No other woman in the world would have this effect on me," I admitted.

Digging my fingers into her silky cheeks, I ground up against her soaking pussy. Pulling her up and down along my length, she moaned. Her pussy lips were massaging my shaft, getting me nice and wet again.

"I want to hear you say it," I said, my voice raspy. "Tell me what you're going to do to me, Eden."

Even though she was stark naked, sliding her wet skin along the length of my cock, she still blushed from the thought of describing it aloud.

"Come on," I encouraged. "Help me out with yet another fantasy."

Her eyes squinched shut as she whispered, "I want you to make love to me right now in your office chair."

Pulling her against me, I kissed her left breast in a big, lazy circle. Then I moved to the right, lapping at her nipple until she quivered.

"That was pretty good," I said. "Except you didn't use any of the bad words." I nodded, trying to appear stern. "I think I need to hear the nasty curse words."

Her adorable laugh surrounded us. I spread her wider, gripping the base of my shaft and gliding it through her juicy pussy lips. Her eyes became hazy as she began to sigh.

"Say it, Eden."

Her hesitation aroused me even more. I couldn't make sense of why. Watching a shy girl decide to be brave turned me on.

Eden paused, hesitating. Then she looked directly at me and whispered, "Eric, I need you to slide that perfect cock into my tight little pussy. I need you to fuck me, right here in your fancy office. Right in front of the windows. I need you to fuck me until I scream."

"Damn, baby," I growled, I sheathed myself inside her with one long, deep thrust. Her shuddering gasp was the hottest thing in the universe.

Kissing her nipples gently, they almost felt heated. Her

hips were restless as she raised and lowered herself, shimmying slightly from side to side.

I'd never felt completely lusty before. Like an animal. Like a raw, feral creature that just needed to fuck.

Eden's back arched slightly with a choppy moan, her uneven noises adding to our pleasure. Holding her hips securely, I dug in, thrusting up into her. But I couldn't really pound her from this position.

Standing, I took one step forward to lay her back across the desk. Her shapely legs wrapped around me instantly.

"I love how big you are," she whispered as I slid inside her deeper, deeper.

"You feel like heaven, baby," I murmured against her ear. "No wonder you were named for paradise."

Pulling out almost completely, I slammed back inside her quick and rough. Her eyes blazed, her fingers digging into the muscles of my shoulders. "How can you make me feel this good?" she whimpered.

"I was meant for you," I said.

A shudder passed through her, and her round ass tightened under my hands, bucking up against me. I could feel that she was rubbing her clit against my skin. Knowing that she was using my body for her pleasure drove me insane.

Her pussy was gripping me so tightly that I could tell she was about to explode. "Should I slow down?" I asked, raking my teeth along her collarbone.

"Never."

"Should I be more gentle?"

"No."

Gripping the back of her hair with my right hand, I tilted her lips to mine, kissing her so hard she whined under me. "You know what I need to hear. Tell me what you want or I'm going to stop."

She was so close that she was twitching. Her fingernails dug into my skin. "Don't stop," she whispered. "Keep fucking me hard. Keep driving that delicious cock into me until I come."

I did as precisely as she commanded, growling, "Then what do you want me to do, baby?"

"Fill me," she choked. "I need..." She couldn't finish her thought. It looked like her body was being shaken from within as a hot flush ran up her cheeks.

Feeling her pussy contracting and releasing around me, I lost my mind, driving deep through her climax. As my cock began to fire thick ropes of cum deep inside her, I growled into our kiss, "You're perfect, Eden. I had no idea how much I needed you."

Then as my hips spasmed harder, I made a completely inhuman sound that I didn't recognize, but it made Eden's eyes light up with bliss.

## 17

---

### EDEN

** Eden's **

On some level, what we had done was a tiny bit wrong. Eric's place of business was not an appropriate place for sex. Even though there was nobody around, and the door was locked, it was a bit sketchy.

Maybe that's why it felt so damn incredible. As we got dressed and Eric led me to the ladies' room so I could freshen up a bit, I couldn't stop grinning. Which made Eric grin. Which made me smile even more.

We were infinitely dorky together. There were so many things about us that just clicked.

I found myself actually questioning Nana's Knowing. It certainly wasn't scientific. It wasn't logical. We hadn't really tracked how many times she had said something that could have been a coincidence. We'd never really tracked how many times something had come true. Or didn't.

When it came to matters of the heart, it was easy to believe in the mystical. It was too easy to give in to fear.

As I met Eric back in the lobby and we headed to the elevator, I wondered if I had believed Nana's prophecy as an excuse to put armor around my heart. There was no way to know if I was ready for a relationship yet. There was no way to know if Eric was really the one. But the only way I would find these things out is if I gave him a fair chance.

Eric waved good night to the security guard, leading us out of the gorgeous lobby and back onto the street. Then he stopped, examining my eyes. "Our genius plan to take things slow took a wrong turn again. Are you okay with that?"

He seemed instantly relieved when I laughed. "Yes. I guess so. We just seem to have an effect on each other, don't we?"

"Absolutely."

A fire truck went by, and we stopped talking for a moment since there was no way to hear over the siren. The red lights flashed in Eric's deep eyes. It really did make him look a bit devilish. That satisfied smirk made him appear truly wicked. The crucial thing I had to admit to myself was that I dearly loved it.

I appreciated the way he was trying to bring me out of my shell. I liked the way he wouldn't take no for an answer when he knew something was right. Because he also analyzed my every reaction, ready to stop if I said a word.

He truly cared about me. A lot. A heck of a lot, for someone I barely knew. There was something strangely magical in the pull we had toward each other. I needed to listen to that more than something my grandmother once muttered.

A devil was a creature who did evil things. I couldn't imagine Eric doing anything evil. Not ever.

When the siren faded away, the sound bouncing off the

office towers, Eric asked, "Where do you live? Would you like me to walk you home, or we could get a cab?"

I'd seen his glamorous home. If we were truly getting to know each other in this extremely fast forward fashion, he might as well see my place. "It's not too far, we could walk to my apartment," I said. I took his hand and we began to walk east.

"Don't worry," Eric said with a chuckle, "I don't expect to stay over. I know that you wouldn't want the devil in your bed."

We stopped at a red light, and I surprised myself by turning to him, running my fingers up the back of his neck as I pulled his lips down to mine. He instantly wrapped his arms around me, and suddenly we were the only two people in the city.

When the light changed, I pulled away and took his hand again. "No self-respecting girl would allow a demon into her bed. But you, on the other hand," I flashed him a saucy wink. "You might be permitted."

I loved how his face was so expressive. I loved the way his fingers gripped mine. We walked so casually and perfectly together. I loved the feeling of falling in love.

When we got to my gray apartment building, I said, "I hope you're not expecting anything posh. It's just a crappy little student apartment."

Eric squeezed my hand. "Crappy? That's pretty extreme language coming from you."

"I guess I've been hanging out with a bad influence," I said. We went up to my sixth-floor apartment in an elevator that went at a normal, slow clunking speed.

As we walked down the hallway to my door, Eric looked around, seeming amused. "I feel like I've gone through a time portal to the eighties," he whispered.

Looking around to the faded patterned carpet, the weirdly dramatic wall sconce lighting, I nodded. "Maybe even the late seventies."

"It's kind of awesome, though," he said with a grin.

He wasn't being polite. He was genuinely appreciative of my lousy apartment building, which was reasonably clean, but definitely old and worn.

After digging in the bottom of my purse for the key, I let us in, and Eric immediately went to the center of the room, turning around slowly and staring.

"If you're planning a photoshoot for one of those gorgeous home magazines, you can save your energy," I laughed.

"I'm taking you in," he said quite seriously. "I know that students make do with whatever furniture they can get their hands on. But you chose that purple star wall hanging. You chose those bright red coffee mugs. Surrounding yourself with things you like is an ingrained human trait."

"A builder and philosopher," I said, kicking off my shoes and dumping my purse on the chair by the front door. Walking past him to the couch, I sat on the side that creaked, since he was certainly heavier than I was.

Eric sat beside me, still analyzing everything while setting a hand on my knee. "A small TV and a giant bookshelf. That is always a good sign." Then he turned to me. "You're in university now. Do you have a part-time job as well?"

"Sort of. I work part-time for my mother, helping her with research and proofreading. In the summers and over breaks, I work for her company full-time. During the school year, I'm able to just update their website and do promotion and stuff from here."

"That's brilliant," he said. He squeezed my knee gently,

giving me a strange smile. "I'm relieved that you're not one of those students who have to work eight part-time jobs, and never sleep, and could never afford to eat. I've seen what some people have to go through, and it's rough."

I was touched that he would even think of such things. "My mother always said that we are not well off, but we are well organized," I smiled. "We did without certain things so that we were in a good place for our education. My older sister actually lived in this apartment when she was going to school, and passed it down to me to avoid the rent hike."

"Clever," Eric grinned.

"I don't know if it's impolite to ask, but were your parents wealthy?" I asked.

Eric gave my knee another squeeze. "I want you to feel free to ask me absolutely anything, at any time. Manners be damned. Okay?"

I nodded. "Okay."

"My parents were..." He made a strange expression, staring down at the chipped coffee table, shaking his head. "Very strange. They named my sister Angelica, hoping that it would bring her the luck of the Angels. And they named me after some weird demon thinking that it would toughen me up."

He raised an eyebrow. "I think it's pretty safe to say that they're a bit unusual."

"That sounds fair."

"They were sort of hippies," he said. "My mother's father was apparently loaded, and gave her an allowance for her entire life, so she never had to work. That gave my dad the opportunity to move us around all the time, chasing his get rich quick schemes."

"Did they ever work normal jobs?" I couldn't resist asking.

Eric rolled his eyes. "Of course not." He turned to me, taking my hands in his. "But there's something to be learned in every single situation we are thrown into. Angie and I learned how to work hard, and save every penny while hiding it from our parents. We learned to work as a team. We put each other through school, then started a company by researching brilliant people who had never been given enough opportunity."

"Are you close with your parents now?" I asked.

He shook his head. "My Dad stopped wanting to be monetarily rich as soon as he saw Angie and I become wealthy. We offered to buy them a house, but Dad shunned us. They moved to some monastery or ashram or something in India."

"Wow."

Eric looked slightly disturbed. "I wish them well on their spiritual journey, whatever it is. I just hope they have enough food from my mother's painting and my father's basket sculptures. The last I heard, that's what they were selling."

"Does your mother still get her allowance?"

He shrugged, with a long low exhale. "My grandparents passed away, so I have no idea. My mother has a brother, apparently, but I've never met him. All I have is her email address, but she only responds once or twice a year."

I squeezed his hands gently. "People lose their families in all sorts of ways. But to have them sort of drift off and disappear. That's awful. I'm sorry."

"I can imagine them waving incense and crystals, having the time of their lives," he said, trying to smile. "They know that they can contact us if they ever need help. That's their choice, I guess."

Eric leaned back on the couch, stretching his arm over

the back to pull me into his shoulder. "It sounds like you're pretty close with your family," he said.

I nodded. "I have some friends who have to call their mothers every single day. Luckily we're not that close." I rolled my eyes while Eric laughed.

"We check in once a week or so. I know that I could call my Mom or Eva in the middle of the night and they would drop everything to help me. They're only an hour away, so it's a comfort knowing that I could run away and stay with either of them for a weekend to recharge."

"What about your grandmother?" He asked. "Do you drop in for tea all the time?"

"I wish," I sighed. "My mother's brother Nick lives in Vancouver, and has two little kids. So Nana moved out to Vancouver to live in a retirement community on the ocean and be with her smallest grandkids."

Eric nodded, his fingers trailing up and down my arm lightly. "Well, I guess you and Eva are able to use the phone to keep in touch with her. Kids would find that tricky. Do you fly out there very often?"

"I wish. Flights are expensive. The only time I can take the time off school is when their prices are jacked because it coincides with breaks."

He leaned in and kissed the top of my hair. "Hopefully your Nana knows how to do video calls?"

I laughed. "Uncle Nick said he was going to teach her. But that was a few months ago. My Mom is actually there visiting her now. I'll text her in the morning to remind her to try."

I saw Eric look over to the giant industrial clock on the wall. "Did you steal that from high school?" he asked.

"Of course not," I said, "Although that would've been cool. I found it in a secondhand store for ten dollars."

"You're naughty," he grinned. "I like naughty. But it's getting kind of late, so I should go."

My hand flashed out, my fingers pressing against his chest. "I don't want you to leave." It was weird that I had spoken without thinking. That was happening far more often around him.

He stared at me, wide eyed. "Eden, are you inviting me to spend the night?"

"I guess so?" I said hesitantly.

My eyes fell closed for a second as his thumb ran along my cheek tenderly. "We just keep mixing everything up, don't we?" he said. "Logically, we know that we should slow things down and just date like normal people."

"You know this doesn't feel normal," I whispered.

Eric nodded. He looked like he was trying to analyze a solution to the problem. "I don't want to be too forward," he said softly. "But I don't want to leave." Leaning in, he brushed his lips against mine, soft as a breeze.

"What if we slept together without sleeping together?" he said with a sassy little grin. "We can snuggle all night, but my shorts will stay on. Deal?"

Just from thinking about him sleeping in my bed with me, my thighs were starting to quiver. But I was fairly certain I could behave myself.

"Deal."

Puttering around my apartment getting ready for bed was a normal routine, but I'd never done it with a man present before. I'd always stayed over at Andy's because he wanted all of his stuff around. Once again I was struck by the fact that he treated me as an inconvenience, whereas Eric was treating me like a precious treasure.

While he was in the washroom, I quickly changed into my pink boy short pajama bottoms, but I wore a pretty camisole instead of my usual ragged gray tank top. I got into bed just before he came out, and he switched off the light, crawling in beside me. It wasn't a large bed, so we immediately spooned.

Twisting over my shoulder, I gave him a kiss. "Thank you for showing me your city block toys," I giggled.

"Baby, you can come and play with my toys anytime you want," Eric chuckled. "Thank you for making a dirty man's fantasy come true."

Snuggling back against him, I tried to fall asleep. But the sexy electric prickle between us soon had me feeling flushed and wanting.

# 18

ERIC

*Goodnight*

Feeling the way Eden's curvy body leaned back into mine was driving me crazy. But just for once, I needed to keep a promise. Well, it wasn't exactly a promise. But it was a statement. No sex tonight.

It was important to me that she knew I wanted to care for her more than I wanted to take care of my own sex drive. She had probably known men who were total pigs. Every woman did. I wanted to be better than all other men for her. I wanted her to understand that her needs came first. Always.

Right now, she needed some attention. My arms were wrapped around her, but it definitely felt like she needed more.

Sliding my hands under her top, I placed them flat on her stomach. Her breath hitched. Her body quivered. My sweet little girl needed something to relax her, and who was I to deny a lady what she needed?

"Aren't you sleepy, baby?"

"Not yet," she whispered.

"Tell me what you need."

I heard that strange, dark tone enter my voice, and wasn't sure what I thought about it until I heard her soft exhale. "I need you to touch me."

My hands began spreading apart across her skin, one moving up and one moving down, sliding into the waistband of her shorts. I moved slower than a glacier. I wanted to tease her, drive her mad with desire. From the way her breath hitched again, and the way her thighs began to quiver back against me, it was certainly working.

After several minutes, I cupped the bottom of her left breast, as my right hand slid slowly between her silky folds.

I caressed her gently, slowly. It was clearly having the desired effect, as she was trembling. My fingertips lightly skimmed along her skin, and I was delighted to find she was absolutely drenched.

Dipping a finger around her entrance, stirring her moisture, I whispered, "Are you wet for me?"

"Always," she breathed.

"Really?" I purred into her ear, squeezing her breast so tightly she gasped. "I like thinking about that. Your body craving mine."

"Yes," she breathed, then she moaned as I slid my middle finger into her wet tunnel.

"You are impossibly sexy," I murmured against her ear. "I've never needed anyone as desperately as I need you."

Her soft whimper as I added a second finger made my cock so hard I thought it was going to crack. But this couldn't be about me.

Gliding my fingers all the way in and out of her wet pussy at a slow, seductive pace, I brought my thumb to her clit, nudging gently in tiny circles.

"Yes," she breathed.

"Yes, what?" I asked. "Yes, you want me to stop now and let you sleep?"

"Don't stop," she whispered quickly. "Please..."

"You know I'm going to make you say it, baby. You know how much that turns me on."

She twisted, looking over her shoulder at me. "Why do you like making me say dirty things?"

I grinned in the near dark. "Because it's sexy as hell thinking of you being so overcome with lust that you lose yourself with me." Her eyes sparkled in the dim light, as I leaned in to kiss her nose. "You're absolutely gorgeous," I said softly. "But turning you into a filthy little vixen is amusing."

"You want to change me?" she asked teasingly.

"Oh no, baby. You're already naughty. I just want you to understand it, and be in touch with it. I want you to let your inner self out."

She started to say something, but I thrust my fingers hard and fast for several strokes. Then I paused, swirling around her entrance without penetrating her. I pulled my thumb from her clit and my hand from her breast, making her whine.

"If you want me to do anything else, you're going to have to remind me what you want."

Eden released a long, agonizing moan that was almost obscenely arousing. "You're such a tease," she said. "You know what I want."

I leaned in to kiss her gently. "I'm a bad man who wants to hear a good girl say dirty words."

This time she barely hesitated. "Eric, please make me come."

"Good girl," I murmured against her ear. "Tell me what you want me to do."

I felt her hesitate again, then she blurted, "Squeeze my breast and pinch my nipple, not too hard."

Having her give me directions was so erotic. "What else do you want, baby?"

"Fuck me with your fingers. Put your thumb on my clit and do those perfect little circles."

I tried to shift my hips so that my raging erection wasn't pressing against her so hard. But she was quivering so violently that she might not have noticed. Plunging my fingers inside her gloriously wet pussy, I kept a slow, steady rhythm as I massaged her clit.

"Your wish will always be my command, Eden," I whispered.

Her head fell back, her hand reached around to grab my thigh. Stretching my shoulder so that I could plunge deeper, her half-strangled moan filled the room. "Oh fuck," she whispered. "Faster... Please..."

I didn't increase my speed. I wanted her climax to be spectacular. "What is it that you want faster?"

"Your fingers," she moaned wildly. "Fuck my pussy faster."

I kissed and nibbled the side of her neck, doing precisely what she wanted. Feeling her sweet body trembling so helplessly against me was a strange thrill.

The urge to care for someone had never been this strong in my life. I needed this amazing girl with me forever. That odd little fact snuck into the back door of my brain when I wasn't paying attention. But it was the absolute truth.

I pounded her wetness with my fingers. I swirled across her skin, pressing deeply into her clit as I pinched her nipple so hard she squealed.

"Come for me, baby," I growled. "Let me hear it."

Her high-pitched shriek of "Oh fuck oh fucking yes!" probably carried through half of the building. Her entire body bucked in shock, then leaned back against me hard while she trembled. Her glorious pussy clenched my fingers tight as her screams turned to moans. After a moment, she seemed to relax, panting slightly.

I kissed along her neck, her shoulder. "That sounded amazing. I need to make you squeal like that every single day."

Eden wriggled so that she was on her back, facing me. She looked slightly dazed. "How do you do that to me?" she asked.

Gripping her ass roughly, I pulled her against me. "I want to give you absolutely everything you need," I said honestly. "I want to be your man. I want you to come to me with every problem so that I can help it go away. I want to do everything I can to make you happy."

She backed away an inch, blinking as she focused on my eyes in the dim light.

Squeezing her ass again, I chuckled. "I know that's way too serious. That's probably a conversation for months down the road."

She placed both of her hands on my chest, not pushing me away, just touching me. "I want to be with you," she said with a sweet giggle. "I do want you to be my guy."

Leaning in, I kissed her gently. Dreamily. "You make me so happy," I murmured. "But you should probably sleep, baby. Don't you have class in the morning?"

She bit her lip, looking up at me. "I think there's something I should likely take care of first."

Her hands began to slip down my chest. I gripped each

wrist, spinning her away from me and pinning her hands with mine against her stomach.

"Sleep," I said softly. "I need my sweet girl to have a well-rested brain so that you can suck up all that important knowledge tomorrow."

"But–"

"Eden, you know that I would never tell you what to do. But right now, I order you to go to sleep."

We laughed together, then settled down, her breathing becoming smoother and slower. Being completely still with Eden in my arms was beautiful. It felt so peaceful, as if everything in the universe was precisely how it was supposed to be.

**19**

---

EDEN

** Flight **

I woke up slowly, not even startled that someone's arms were around me. Eric felt right. Even when I was unconscious, my body and mind were completely comfortable with him. Somehow, that said something important.

I turned to look at his unbelievably handsome face, still asleep. He looked so peaceful.

It was funny how I had always feared change, but somehow not with him. I'd always been terrified when I wasn't in control of a situation. But when Eric took control of me, only wonderful things happened. I'd always been quiet and shy, yet here he was, encouraging me to speak up and become a bit louder. It was adorable that he didn't want to change me. Only enhance me.

After seeing so many friends change for the worse once they'd been dating a guy for a while, this connection was positively inspiring.

Stretching slightly, I wondered whether I should bother

going to my ten am lecture. It was on a topic I already had completely covered, so there was really no reason to go. I had an essay due for the end of the day. It would probably take about two more hours of writing, and one hour of proofing.

Watching Eric's eyes slowly flicker open, I somehow knew that he would tell me to put my schoolwork first. Even though I would have loved to spend the day with him instead.

"Hey," he said softly. "How is the most beautiful girl in the world?"

Rolling so that I could snuggle into him tighter, I said, "I have no idea. But I am doing just fine with this sexy man beside me."

His enormous grin was adorable. "Should I go put the coffee on, or should we do some very important snuggling first?" he asked.

Before I could tell him that snuggling was always more important even though coffee was the essence of life, I was interrupted by my phone ringing.

Sitting up quickly, I grabbed it, glancing at Eric. He placed his finger over his lips, indicating that he wouldn't make a peep.

As I answered it, I saw that it was my sister Eva. "Hey, what's–"

"Mom's in the hospital, she broke her leg," Eva blurted.

"What?" I sat up straighter.

"She's okay, I think, but it might mess up her new hip."

"Sassafras," I muttered through grit teeth. Eric reached out to place a hand on my leg reassuringly. It was comforting to know that he was right here with me.

"They're going to operate today, to reset her leg and put pins in it or something, to make sure it's stable and doesn't pull her hip out of alignment," Eva said. She sounded frantic, speaking way too fast like she did when she was upset.

"Take a breath," I said. "Is she still in Vancouver?"

"Yes. I'd go to her, but we have a gigantic release on Friday. My team would kill me if I even thought of taking off."

"I'll go to her," I said immediately. "Text me the name of her hospital, her doctor, whatever you've got. I'll get on a plane as soon as I can."

"Thanks, Eden," she said. "I can't stand the thought of her being there without one of us."

"I'll talk to you soon," I said, ending the call.

Turning to Eric, I said, "I'm so sorry."

He grabbed my hand. "Don't be sorry. Be clear. What happened and what do you need?"

"My mother broke her leg," I said, hearing my voice quavering. "She just got a hip replacement six months ago, so they have to operate and straighten it out or something so that it doesn't injure the new hip."

"You said she's in Vancouver right now?"

I nodded, my mind starting to fire at full speed. "Yes. So I'm sorry to take off on you, but I'm going to have to book a flight, and pack. And, I guess get a hotel room near the hospital if it's far away from Uncle Nick."

Eric squeezed my hand. "Take a big breath in, then blow it out slowly."

While I did that, he grabbed his phone from the nightstand and made a call. "Good morning Patricia. I'm going to need the plane this morning. To Vancouver. Two passengers, as quickly as possible." He paused. "Yes, thank you. I don't know which hotel yet, I'll text you when I have an approximate location. Thanks."

I snapped my mouth shut from where it had fallen open. "You can just... Do that?"

"Yes. Get dressed while we talk."

We both got up and started pulling our clothes on. "Do you want me to come with you?" he asked. "I can send you on your own if you'd prefer, but I'd like to be there for you if you want me."

"Don't you have to work?"

He smiled sweetly. "The essential things I can all do from my phone. Patricia will cancel any meetings today, and keep me on top of everything."

"Wow."

He reached across the corner of the bed to grab my hand. "Eden, don't think about my work. Let me help. Do you want me to come with you?"

I nodded. "Yes. Thank you."

Eric stroked my hair. "Don't worry. Your mom is going to be fine. They have great hospitals there."

I glanced at my phone, seeing that Eva had sent me a text. "She's at Vancouver General Hospital," I said.

"Good. Pack some clothing, and whatever you need to survive. Like your laptop for school. Anything else, I can buy you while we're there."

He grabbed his phone again. "Patricia? I'll need a room at a hotel very close to Vancouver General." He turned to me. "What's your mom's full name?"

"Penelope Palmer."

"Did you catch that? Please contact the hospital to make sure that she's upgraded to the best private room they have. And a private nurse, if possible. Thank you."

I couldn't believe what I was hearing. I was also distracted from trying to pull my tiny rolling suitcase from the top shelf of the closet. Before I could blink, Eric was there lifting it down as if it weighed nothing.

"Thank you so much," I started, I can't even–"

Eric placed a finger on my lips. "Let's talk on the plane. For now, grab everything you need for the next several days. Bring your books and school work."

I barely knew what was happening, but I was being hurried out the door. As I locked up, Eric took my suitcase and shoulder bag.

"Will we stop by your place to get some things?" I asked.

He shook his head, smiling slightly as I headed for the elevator. "I have a suitcase already on the plane, and a spare laptop. I'm good."

"Oh. Wow."

"Angie and I never know when we might have to make a break for it to show up early for a presentation," he explained. "So we each have a tiny closet on the plane, just in case."

I didn't recall him calling for a cab, but there was one in front of the building. I'd never been to the little island airport before. Even though I was stressed out of my mind, the ninety-second ferry ride was almost fun.

My head was spinning as Eric led me to a gleaming white plane, and up the steps.

"Hello again, Mr. Stone. Welcome aboard." A nice motherly lady in a sharp gray suit dress guided us aboard.

"Hi, Andrea. Sorry for the rush. This is Eden."

The woman's eyes lit up. "What a wonderful name. Please, have a seat anywhere you like. Captain Nichols is your pilot today."

My luggage was stowed and I was seated in a giant leather chair. Eric had given me the window seat, and sat close beside me.

"Can I get you anything before takeoff?" Andrea asked politely.

"No, thanks," Eric said quickly. "We'll worry about that once we get going. We have a hospital to get to in a hurry."

"Oh," Andrea said, immediately concerned as she realized this was not a flight merely for pleasure, or a business meeting. She dashed into the cockpit, coming out just a moment later. "I've informed the Captain that this is a rush, and he will do everything in his power to, as he put it, 'run some red lights on the way'."

I laughed too hard, but I really did need a break in the tension.

It was sweet that after Andrea checked my seatbelt and disappeared to the front of the plane, Eric checked my belt himself. "Do you fly very often?" he asked.

I shook my head. "Only four trips to Vancouver and back. Certainly never in a private jet," I said, looking around wide-eyed. "And certainly not at the drop of a hat like this." I picked up Eric's hand from the armrest between us. "Thank you," I said sincerely. "This means so much to me."

"I don't have a lot of experience with normal families," Eric said. "But I feel like you should do everything in your power to comfort an ailing parent, right?"

"Yes, but this isn't in my power," I said, waving again to the gorgeously designed interior and plush seating.

"It's in your power now," he said gently. "You're an important part of my life, Eden. Everything I have is yours."

I had no idea what on earth to say to that.

Then he shook his head with a loud sigh. "Dammit, I'm sorry. It's too much too fast. I know. This is why I suck at relationships. I don't know how to think before I speak."

I heard the engines kick in with a low rumble. Instantly I

gripped his hand tight. "I think you're doing pretty darn well at this relationship so far," I said. My voice sounded strained.

The deep, powerful chugging from beneath our feet changed. It sounded like a supercar being forced to drive one mile an hour. Like it was barely being held back.

Eric released my hand to clasp onto the other one, so that he could wrap his arm around me tightly. "This is the best company, with the best pilots," he said softly. "As soon as we are up and away, we can have coffee and breakfast. Alright?"

The plane turned, then began zipping down the runway much faster than I could have expected. Maybe it just felt different since I was used to huge airbus vehicles.

"I might need that coffee spiked hard," I muttered, gritting my teeth.

"No problem," he chuckled. "Your only mission for the next five hours is your schoolwork, and telling me how to behave around your family."

I felt the wheels leave the ground with a lurch that dropped the pit of my stomach a couple of feet. My involuntary squeal made Eric laugh. "Breathe, baby. It's fine. I've got you."

Before I could think, he was kissing me gently, his lips barely hovering against mine. Then he sat back, just holding me while I calmed down.

He dropped my hand to pull out his phone, flipping through a few quick texts.

"Wait, you can use your phone here?"

He grinned. "Another little perk of flying private."

His eyes were so deep and sharp as they darted around the screen. "Your mother is doing fine," he said. "She's been moved to a private room, with a private nurse. She's being prepped for surgery right now, and they estimate it will only take around three and a half hours."

"Oh. Thank you."

"That's great," he said brightly. "By the time she is coming around, you'll be there by her side."

I grinned, leaning in to kiss his cheek. "Thank you."

"You are extremely welcome," he smiled. Then he straightened up, giving his shoulders a shake. "Time to get down to business."

As if on cue, a tiny ping sounded, and Andrea came toward us. "Coffee to start?" she asked.

"Yes," Eric said, "But throw a half shot of Kahlúa into Eden's to steady her nerves."

Andrea chuckled, nodding. "No problem."

"Then if you could please grab my laptop from the back closet drawer, we're going to have to get to work."

"Certainly, sir."

Eric turned to me and said, "I'd like you to stay buckled in at all times, okay?"

I nodded, as he unfastened his belt and went to get my shoulder bag from the front closet. I'd never had anyone be so protective of me.

We were soon set up on our tray tables, in our own weird mobile office, as Andrea brought the coffee.

"Set your phone three hours ahead now," he suggested. "It's nearly nine here, so it's six am Vancouver time. Better to do it now to reset your brain."

"Oh right, thanks." I fussed with my phone, relieved that he'd think of that. I guess he was a lot more accustomed to traveling than I was. It was also sweet to feel so cared for, like he was looking out for me.

"What assignments do you have due today?" Eric asked.

I rolled my eyes. "I'm nearly done an essay, but I don't know if I have the attention span to proofread it on a plane."

"Is it okay to have someone else proofread it? It's just for typos really, right?"

"Yes."

Eric grabbed his phone. "What's your email?"

I told him, shocked at how fast his thumbs flew across the screen. Then he grabbed my laptop, typing a note. "That's Lesley's email. She's one of my interns. Send your essay to her. She can proof it, fix any typos, then forward it straight to your professor, or whatever you like."

I started to protest, but he held up his hand. "Patricia and I have been desperate to try to find enough projects to keep two interns busy this month. There's just been a lull in the workload. So this is actually extremely convenient for me."

I tried to raise an eyebrow suspiciously but just burst into giggles. "You are like a genie who grants wishes," I laughed.

"Sure, you can call me Gene if you want to. Just get writing." He snapped his fingers briskly. "Twenty minutes of hard work, then we get a fabulous breakfast as a reward."

Opening up the documents I needed, I took a sip of coffee, then shook my head. "I can't believe I have an assistant on standby to help with my essay. I feel so completely spoiled."

Eric nudged my shoulder with his. "Many hands make light work, and all that," he said. "Hell, how do you think I found out which bar in the city serves a Blue Beach?"

My head swiveled, staring at him. "You had your interns stalk me?"

His eyes flew wide as if he realized he may have made a mistake. "No, not you. Not anything personal about you.

Just, you know, which place happened to serve that drink," he said lamely.

I froze. What the blazes does one say to that?

His eyes tightened and he looked extremely worried. Still looking at me, he picked up his pen. "Psst," he hissed. "Do you think she'll believe that I really needed a project for the interns that day?"

He cocked his head as if listening, then nodded. "I know. It sounds really awful. But I'm trying to make up for it now. Do you think that counts?" He paused, nodding. "Only time will tell. Yeah, you're probably right. Best to just get back to work and pretend that didn't happen."

Eric nodded again, then slowly turned back to his own laptop, opening what seemed to be a highly secure email program.

I laughed, shaking my head, as I tried to focus on my work.

Yet it was hard to put that aside. True, I had freaked out and not answered his messages, and he had no other clues to find me. But should a man really track a woman down like that?

It was in a public place, and they were lots of people around. Everyone has heard horror stories of creepers showing up at their apartment door, or their back window. Eric had come to me at my local pub, simply asking to chat for a moment.

It was weird, and a bit extreme, but I thought it was relatively acceptable. As long as it never went farther than that.

He was right though. He was certainly going above and beyond the call for me right now, so I tried to put it out of my mind.

No matter how much help I had, I really did have to write the essay myself.

# 20

ERIC



It was an incredible relief when Eden laughed about my method of tracking her down. Even if the merriment didn't quite reach her eyes.

Yet I couldn't think about that at the moment. Angie was freaking out that I was missing the meeting for the first design drafts of a new tower we were building. Luckily I was a bit anal-retentive about getting things done in advance. I was able to direct her to where Patricia had the blueprints and presentation materials all ready to go.

ANGIE SENT ME A TEXT, and I could almost hear how confused she was.

*A: Patricia said that you took the jet to Vancouver? What's wrong? Did the Wrenwyck project go sideways?*

*E: Everything's fine. A friend's mother is in the hospital, and she had no way to get there in time to meet her mother after surgery.*

*A: E, are you being a good Samaritan? Or are you trying to impress that girl? Sometimes I can't tell with you.*

*E: I'll have you know that the charming lady I am with is swiftly becoming the love of my life. She needs help right now, so I'm helping her.*

I saw those three dots hovering for longer than I expected.

*A: Wow. You actually used the L-word. I'm rather impressed.*

*In that case, tell me if there is anything I can do to help. I'll take care of things here. Stay in touch.*

*E: Thanks, sis. You are a superstar.*

*A: Never forget that.*

I wanted to mention to Eden how alike she and Angie were, but she seemed completely focused on typing away at her project.

It was interesting watching her work. She would type

like crazy for about a minute, then freeze, staring into space. Although her head was tilted slightly toward the window, it was clear that she wasn't watching the scenery below. She was completely zoned out, in a trance while she thought very hard about whatever she was writing. It was amazing to see her in a completely different light.

I realized that I would soon be seeing her with her family, which would be yet another side of her.

Although I didn't believe in the supernatural, I couldn't help politely asking the universe to make sure her mother was all right.

I had been far too pushy already, but I was desperately hoping to meet this mysterious grandmother. It seemed like everyone tiptoed around her unexplainable prophecies. I wanted to ask her flat out. Since I was outside of the circle, perhaps I could do this in a way that seemed charming instead of rude.

Strangers could often ask stupid questions and be forgiven because they didn't know the rules yet. I would have to rely on that train of thought to get through it.

It was incredibly important that her mother and grandmother like me. I needed them to see me as a good partner for Eden. It was inevitable that we would end up married, with kids, and living our own little happily ever after.

The wonderful thing is, I'd never pictured anything specific in my perfect home life. So Eden could make all of the major decisions, like where we should live, and what sort of house we should buy. I wanted to give her absolutely everything.

She didn't seem to care about money, which was certainly a breath of fresh air. She wasn't the type to be greedy, or wasteful. She wasn't the type to put on airs.

After about half an hour, Andrea approached cautiously. "Breakfast?"

Eden looked at me hopefully. "Yes?"

"Absolutely," I said, quickly stowing both of our laptops.

As always, Andrea outdid herself, serving fresh blueberry pancakes, scrambled eggs, hash browns, and fresh fruit smoothies.

"This is one of the many reasons why Andrea is the absolute best," I loudly told Eden while Andrea was setting out extra napkins.

"Thank you, Mr. Stone," she said with a grin.

Then she turned to Eden. "Although I did spike your coffee, if you are a nervous flyer, I can also offer you mimosas, champagne, wine, or pretty much anything else." She flashed a wide smile. "Captain Nichols will notify us in advance if he foresees any turbulence, but the last I heard it should be smooth sailing."

"I think I'm fine for now," Eden said. "Thank you so much."

Andrea disappeared, and Eden turned to me. "Do you find it weird having people serve you?"

I took a huge gulp of my smoothie while nodding. "Yes, sometimes. On a flight, it's expected. I know some people have assistants around them at all times, but personally, I find that a bit weird. I have a cleaning lady that comes on Tuesdays. That's enough for me," I shrugged.

She seemed to be relieved. "Good."

"I'm looking forward to meeting your family," I said as she started with her pancakes. "I'm curious to see what sort of people you came from."

Eden looked delighted that I was truly interested. "My mother has worked as a researcher and script fact-checker most of her life. When she had to have her hip replaced, she semi-retired, just doing a bit of freelance work now. Plus it can be done through email, so she doesn't have to run around as much."

"That's great," I said. "So she could stay with your uncle a bit and work remotely if she wants to heal up for a few more weeks before she flies home."

Eden nodded, then her bottom lip began to tremble.

"Oh my God, baby, I'm so sorry. She's going to be fine."

She looked up at me, her eyes a bit glassy, and I took her hand. "Okay, I'll be honest," I said. "It's going to suck a bit. Surgery always does. But they have good painkillers, and she can take her time healing, right? Her only job is to lay around and let people care for her right now."

She gave me a brave little smile. "Thank you for thinking of getting her a private nurse," she said softly. "That will probably be really helpful."

"Patricia sent me a brochure on the company. Apparently, they care for the patients both mentally and physically. So if your mom wants to be left alone to read or rest, that's fine. But if she wants to chat or play cards, she'll always have company whenever she needs it."

"You're amazing," she whispered softly.

I shook my head. "Not really. But you can go ahead and think that if you like, and I highly encourage it." I winked. "The honest truth is, I got super lucky. Then I worked my ass off, and I became even luckier. Now I get to share some of that. That makes me ridiculously happy."

Eden's smile warmed my heart. All I wanted was to care for her and make her happy.

Now that I had a moment to think about it though, I hoped that I wasn't being too pushy. The worst thing that could happen was to accidentally become a real stalker. The bad guy. An abstract demon who turned out to be bad for her instead of good.

Maybe it was fear, since I'd never been in a real relationship before. Or perhaps it was fear because Eden seemed so delicate. A bit timid. As if she wasn't quite sure yet where she stood in the world.

A pushy, domineering man would be the worst thing for a nice young girl. I would never want to inadvertently guide her in a direction she didn't want to go. I would never want to tell her what to do.

But I already had. I'd told her to ignore her grandmother's comment. I'd gently pushed her into giving us another chance. Just because it felt completely right to me didn't mean that it was right for her.

No matter what happened, I'd have to keep my eyes open, and my emotions in check. The underworld that was my namesake could be the hell on earth I'd have to go through if I ever hurt Eden.

**21**

---

EDEN

** Long White Hallways **

I t was a huge relief to send off my essay, knowing that fresh eyes would be going over it before it was handed in. This gave me a little time to listen to quiet music and try to compose myself before we landed.

While I was writing, I had to focus. Now there was a bit of space for the thoughts to spin around my mind like a tipsy tornado.

Eric seemed to always be in problem-solving mode. I found that extremely interesting. He wasn't aggressive about it, just forthright. He wasn't obtrusive, he was used to taking charge of the situation, and creating a positive outcome.

Perhaps it was from clawing his way to the top while he was building his business. Or some people are just hard-wired in different ways.

I'd always been the person to sit still and think things through for hours and days before making a decision. I would never be known as a person of action. It was not my nature.

Maybe it was because I was usually lost in books and quiet thoughts. Maybe it was that standing up for myself was terrifying.

No matter how my mind functioned naturally, Eric seemed to be excellent at nudging me out of my shell. He wasn't demanding, he was playful about it. I knew that I was safe to tell him no at any time. Sometimes I just wanted to please him.

And I dearly wanted to find that part of myself that jumped into action without endless pondering.

Some people can just go with their guts. I don't think I've ever trusted my gut. Everything got tangled up in a wave of nervous tension.

Like knowing that Eric had been strangely aggressive in pursuing me, even calling in help. I honestly didn't know whether that was admirable, or strange. I didn't know if it was a red flag. We felt so right together that it seemed that something so bizarre should be forgiven.

Perhaps it was my paranoia, but the first month of my last relationship I felt on top of the world as well. Not even a quarter as wonderful as I did now, but it was a high at the time. I hoped that my dark thoughts and nervous ways didn't let bad things creep into what could be everything I'd ever dreamed of.

As Andrea gave me some gum to chew during landing, Eric held my hand tightly. No matter what I thought of our relationship overall, I was extremely glad he was here to take care of me. The thought of going to see my mother in the hospital was completely freaking me out.

A town car was already waiting for us on the tarmac. I didn't even know where we were going, but he guided us to the hospital and already knew exactly where my mother's room was.

"I got a text that the surgery went well," he said gently, leading me along. "She just came out of recovery, and was wheeled to her room twenty minutes ago." It was a huge relief that he was so on top of everything.

As we walked down a long white hallway, Eric kept an arm around me. I looked up to see him watching my face. I shrugged slightly. "Yeah, I know. I'm one of those people who get jumpy in hospitals."

He stroked my back gently. "It's okay. Your only job is to chat with your Mom for a while, and let her know you're here for her. I will take care of absolutely everything else."

"Thank you," I whispered, wondering why I was instantly teary so easily. It was probably stress.

Mom was a bit older when she had me, and had always been a little fragile. She was easily sick or injured, but this was likely the worst trip yet.

"Remember," he said as we approached the end of the hall, "She just came out of recovery, so she might be asleep, or groggy, or," he grinned down at me, "High as a kite. Anesthetic affects people in different ways. So don't be alarmed if she's loopy."

I nodded, then we were standing in front of the door of a private room.

Eric hesitated, which was rather unlike him. "I'm pretty sure they only allow one visitor at a time," he said. "And this would be a very strange way for her to meet a stranger. I'll be sitting right here," he said, pointing to a row of chairs. "You take your time, okay?"

Ignoring the two nurses in green scrubs walking by us, I stretched up to give him a kiss. "Thank you," I said again.

He gave me a hug, then set his hands on my shoulders. "It's time for you to be a tough chick," he smiled.

I nodded, then took a few tentative steps through the half-open door.

My mother looked pale, and at least ten years older, lying motionless in the bed. Unlike any hospital room I'd seen previously, this one was nicely decorated like a hotel, with warm lighting instead of ugly fluorescents.

A woman in purple scrubs was sitting in a corner chair, and she jumped up immediately. "Hello," she said in a gentle voice that was nearly a whisper. "You must be Eden. I'm Katy, your mother's nurse."

"How is she?" I asked, matching her quiet tone.

She was almost as old as my mother, and had lovely gentle energy around her. Her instant smile made me feel a lot better. "She's doing really well," Katy said. "She was talking a bit when they transferred her from recovery to this room, but then she closed her eyes again. It's completely normal. People drift in and out for a while."

"And the surgery went well?" I asked.

"Absolutely. Dr. Armstrong said that everything went perfectly. Obviously, she needs to stay off it for several weeks, then there will be a bit of physio to build her back up. Then she'll be walking around pretty much like normal."

She cocked her head, looking at me carefully, and lowering her voice even more. "Your mother wasn't a long-distance runner, or a ballroom dancer or anything like that, was she?"

I shook my head. "No, she was a bookworm. She liked long slow walks, but that's about as athletic as she got."

Katy nodded with relief. "Then she'll be absolutely fine. She'll be back to long walks in a few months."

"Eden?" A weak voice rasped from the bed.

I rushed to Mom's side, taking her hand. "Hi," I said gently.

She blinked slowly, then stared at me. "I can't believe you're here."

"Mrs. Palmer, do you feel like sitting up a little more?" Katy asked.

Mom nodded, and Katy raised the head of the bed and arranged her pillows perfectly. It was wonderful to see that Mom would be taken care of completely.

"There's water right here if she needs it, but only a little at first. I'll be in the hallway if you need me for anything," Katy said, leaving us alone.

"So, breaking my leg is a great way to get you out here to visit your grandmother," Mom chuckled weakly.

"No fair," I rolled my eyes. "You know how much it costs to fly out here."

Mom's face fell. "Oh, I'm so sorry, Eden."

"It's actually okay," I grinned. "A friend of mine flew me here in his company's private jet."

Mom gave herself a shake, sitting up straighter. She was looking a bit more clear. "Friend? Is this a friend of the male persuasion?"

Drat this perfect lighting. There was no way she didn't see me blush furiously. Mom laughed a tiny bit. "What's his name?"

"Eric. I'll tell you all about him when you're a bit stronger and not hopped up on goofy juice or whatever they used on you." I pulled a chair over, then gripped her hand again. "I hope it wasn't too terrible."

Mom released a long low sigh, rolling her eyes. "The worst thing is it was my own bloody fault."

"Everyone trips sometimes, Mom."

"Yes, but I had a warning."

There was something in her tone that pointed out

precisely what she meant, but I asked anyway. "What sort of warning?"

"I was at your grandmother's for tea. She did that little zone out thing she does, and she said, 'It's okay to be hurt, you've got to share it with those who care'."

"That could mean absolutely anything," I said.

She gave me a flat stare. "The day before, I had twisted my ankle a bit. I was cooking at Nick's house, and sort of tripped over my own feet, landing on the side of my ankle. It hurt like heck. I knew I should have asked him to finish dinner, but I didn't want to be a bother since I was staying at his place. If I had sat down and put ice on it, it probably would have healed within a few hours."

I shook my head, knowing exactly what she meant. Much like me, my mother never wanted to rock the boat, or create waves. We never wanted to be a bother.

"So the next day, Nick called for me to come downstairs to help him with something. In my rush, my ankle turned and I missed a step." She winced at the memory. "The pain was crazy, but knowing that it was my own stupid fault scared me even more."

"It wasn't your fault, Mom."

She gave me that look. That special mother expression with one partially raised eyebrow that stated she knew I was full of crap. "Our family understands that you don't go against The Knowing," she said, lowering her voice to a whisper. "We don't ignore those unusual little messages."

"There's absolutely no scientific evidence of psychic powers ever proven," I said, trying to sound more sure than I was.

"Well, the proof is in the pudding," she said. "Or in this case, the broken leg."

She squeezed my hand hard, looking at me intently.

"Eden, promise me. Promise me that you will always obey Nana's whispers."

My eyes snapped shut and I felt my face clench.

"Oh god, Eden... What have you done?"

Forcing myself to look into her eyes, she was positively horrified. "Did you do something that was against... You know?"

I couldn't look at her, staring down at our hands. "Not quite, technically," I said. "But what she said was really abstract, and it could be taken so many ways. And the thing she was talking about isn't even really a real thing," I babbled. "Like, a weird old version of a name isn't the name someone goes by, so that doesn't make it real. So you could say that..."

"Eden." I looked up to see her face like thunder. "We don't go against The Knowing. Bad things always happen. Remember when your sister broke her wrist? Remember when... well, you know."

"I know, but–"

"Did you not stop to think for one second that it might..." She stopped herself mid-sentence, shaking her head. "No, that's ridiculous. I'm sorry."

My throat nearly closed. "What were you going to say?" I choked. I felt my back freeze, then my core. She couldn't be saying what I think she was implying.

She laid back a bit, her eyes drooping.

"Mom, are you in pain?"

"No, I'm too dopey to be in pain. But I think I should rest."

"Okay," I said. "Would you like me to come back later tonight?"

She squeezed my hand tightly. "You've just flown all this way. Why don't you have a big dinner and sleep, and come join me for breakfast in the morning? I'll likely make a lot more sense by then."

"Alright."

I stood up and kissed her forehead. "You be a good girl for nurse Katy now," I said, mimicking her voice.

She jokingly reached out as if she were trying to smack my shoulder. "Thank you for coming out here, Eden."

"Anytime. Rest well."

As I turned to leave, I felt like I was trying to push through a brick wall. My feet didn't want to move. My breath was rapid and awkward. My heart was racing unevenly.

Once I walked out into that hallway, I was going to have to break up with Eric and never see him again.

I would have thought that knowledge would cause me to burst into tears. Instead, I felt like I'd been electrocuted. There was a weird hum in one ear, and my skin didn't fit around my joints quite right.

Shuffling one shoe in front of the other, my stomach tightened. I'd have to find a way to get through the next few minutes. Then the next few. One breath at a time, through lips that could never, ever kiss Eric again.

**22**

---

ERIC

As I waited in the hallway for Eden, I was extremely glad that I could get her here in time to visit with her mother. I didn't know much about surgeries and hospitals. But everyone who has been through it mentioned that having visitors was incredibly important.

I could see that being surrounded by strangers would be unnerving. People you are familiar with help you feel grounded. At least, that seemed to be the case.

When the nurse came out of Penelope's room, I introduced myself and gave her my business card in case there were any difficulties. She thanked me and went to the nurses' station two doors down. A few minutes later, I heard an older man ask the nurses for Penelope Palmer's room.

"She has a visitor at the moment," Katy said. "But you can wait right here if you like."

"Thanks. Is there any way you can tell me how she ended up with a private room? We can't afford that."

I stood up, catching his eye as I walked toward him. "Eric

Stone," I said, extending my hand. "You must be Eden's Uncle Nick."

"Yes, I am." He looked confused.

"I'm a friend of Eden's. Don't worry, the private room and nurse are completely taken care of."

"Thank you," he said, clearly looking me up and down.

I always tried to look as subtle as possible, but if someone had a sharp eye, they would probably notice my watch and my shoes. Maybe even that my designer suits were custom fit. I didn't try to walk around announcing that I was extraordinarily wealthy, but if someone was looking for it, the signs were fairly obvious.

"So, a friend of Eden's," he said. "Since her father's not here anymore, am I to be the one to give you the third degree?"

I chuckled. "If you like, sure."

He peppered me with questions regarding my work, my family, where I lived, and my hobbies. Each answer seemed to either impress or satisfy him.

Then he shrugged. "Well, sounds good enough for me, I suppose."

I looked up as Eden came into the hallway. "Hey, how did it go?" I asked softly.

She nodded, looking a bit spaced out. "Mom is good, I think. Katy said that she could probably go home in a few days."

Eden looked up and blinked as she realized we weren't alone, and gave her uncle a little hug hello. "Uncle Nick, would it be easier for you if Mom goes to your place, or to Nana's?"

"I'll ask her," he said. "Either one is fine with me. Is it okay if I go in now?"

"Sure, but she should take a nap after you say hello."

"No problem."

As soon as Nick was gone, I took Eden's hand. "Maybe we should get you some dinner," I said.

She seemed clenched. Her shoulders looked tight and uncomfortable.

"First, let's get you out of this hospital, all right?"

She nodded quickly, and I led her out of the hospital and across the street to a park. I didn't know whether she actually panicked from being in hospitals, but being surrounded by a few trees and a bit of grass was usually helpful for any sort of anxiety.

"Maybe a few slow, deep breaths," I suggested, holding her hand as we sat close together.

There was something intense churning through her mind. It was almost visible. A dark cloud of something downright creepy.

"I didn't tell you how my Dad died, did I?" she asked softly.

"No. I didn't want to pry. But I'm ready to listen."

Eden stared down at her shoes, grinding her toe slowly into the dirt. "The last time Dad visited Nana five years ago, she stared up at the ceiling and whispered, 'Never let yourself get out of range'."

She paused for a minute, then began talking quickly. "Of course he just thought that it meant he shouldn't bite off more than he could chew, or something abstract like that. He never believed in her whispers. He went fishing with his best friend, and they were out of cell phone range. Dad had a heart attack. Dave couldn't call an ambulance, and had to paddle back to the car, drag Dad into it, and drive to a hospital. By the time they got there, Dad was unconscious and it was too late."

"Oh my god, sweetheart. I'm so sorry," I murmured, stroking her hand gently with my thumb. "That's terrible."

Eden nodded. "Sometimes heart attacks just happen. I would have been able to handle that. But Mom, Eva, and I have had a hard time dealing with the fact that he should have known better."

"You blame him for accidentally canoeing out of cell phone range? The message wasn't exactly crystal clear."

"I know." Eden looked so frustrated and angry and heart wrenchingly sad all at once. "But it happened yet again. Mom ignored the whispers and broke her leg. And she seems to think that it might have been extra bad because I ignored it as well."

She looked over at me, her bottom lip trembling. "Didn't I, Erlik?"

Her use of that name stabbed me through the heart with a blade of ice. "You can't think that us being together hurt your mother?" I whispered.

"I don't know. But I think Mom believes it."

"That's not the name on my business cards," I said quickly. "It's not a name I use day to day. It's not really my name." I shook my head. "Dammit, if only I'd put my name in your phone as 'Eric the guy who is already falling for you', all of this could have been avoided."

"Is it the name on your driver's license?" she asked.

I hung my head. "Yes."

Eden turned, releasing my hand, and leaning slightly away from me. "You'll never understand how sorry I am," she said in a weak, quivering voice. "But if you, or anyone else got hurt because of this, I would never forgive myself."

She stood up, her hands clenching and twitching. "I need to be alone for a bit. Thank you so much for everything you've done for me. I feel awful leaving you after everything you're paying for–"

"Don't even think about that," I said. "I'm just happy your mom is being cared for. But please Eden, I never want to stop taking care of you. Helping you. Being with you."

"I can't," she choked, taking a step away from me. "I can't hurt you. I don't want to hurt myself, but that's less important. So I can't see you again."

I just stared at her. Her beautiful lips were twitching. Her lovely eyes refused to look up into mine, as she blinked frantically to hold back the tears.

"What if I got you your own hotel room, and we discussed this in a day or two?" I asked gently.

She shook her head. "No. I can't trust myself. Eric, I... Feel so much for you that walking away feels like shredding myself into pieces. But it's the only choice."

Eden took two more steps back, as if she could feel how much I needed to hold her.

"Thank you for everything. Take care of yourself." She turned and ran. I watched helplessly as she went down the street.

Once she was out of sight, I stood up and went to the row of taxis at the side of the hospital. Jumping in, I gave him an address.

There was no way in heaven or hell that I was going to lose the girl of my dreams because of some superstitious nonsense unless I had proof that it was real. There was only one way to find out.

**23**

---

EDEN

*＊ Nana ＊*

I knew that a cup of tea with my grandmother always made things better. This time, I needed it more than ever.

I found the most direct bus route to take me to Nana's condo. Staring out the window along the way, I couldn't even enjoy the beautiful Vancouver scenery. I felt completely gutted. Not just hollow, but as if I'd been scraped out.

At the time, breaking up with Andy because he was about to dump me anyway was the end of the world. Now I could see that was like comparing a hangnail to tumbling off a cliff.

Eric made my heart race like never before. Now it felt like my heart had disintegrated, leaving behind a residue of black tar. Possibly poisonous.

The worst thing of all was that he might never understand. I wasn't just doing this for my own safety, it was primarily for his.

I knew that listening to whispered outbursts and trying to live your life by them might seem illogical. But my family had seen far too many of these prophecies come true. When you're faced with evidence again and again, you have to accept it. It's always going to be there.

Getting off the bus, I walked two blocks, trying to breathe in some fresh air to clear myself. I couldn't let Nana see how upset I was.

Tomorrow I would figure out how to help Mom for a few days, then get home. Tomorrow, I would figure out how to attempt to patch myself back together well enough to take care of everything. In a few days, I could compose an email or text to Eric, thanking him for everything.

As I entered the lobby of Nana's building, I said good morning to several sweet white-haired ladies who were all reading books on plush couches. It was funny that I'd never seen the seating in a building lobby being used before. It was lovely that they were social during their quiet reading time.

I took the slow elevator up to the fourth floor, while I thought about being alone again. Sure, being alone was a lot better than being with Andy, at the end. In the beginning, I was deliriously happy from the thought of always having someone to call.

I didn't want to be a fragile girl. But there was a great comfort having a man around if I needed protection. Or comfort. A little voice in the back of my head screamed, 'Or a private plane to visit your mother in an emergency.'

The knowledge that I was a complete jerk rattled around my mind heavily. After everything Eric had done for me, I broke up with him. I could only hope that after some time had passed, he would understand that I was doing it for his own safety as well as mine.

Walking down the pristine cream-colored hallway, I felt absolutely nauseated knowing that I had hurt him. There was so much to love about him. So much to still learn. So many possibilities.

Being forced to shut all of this down made my skin crawl. Yet I knew it was right. It was the only safe thing to do. My stomach churned since we had flown together, knowing now what may have happened.

Taking a deep, clearing breath, I smiled hard, trying to relax my face. I had to have a bright expression. Nana might be upset that Mom was in the hospital, so I couldn't put any more stress on her plate right now.

Knocking on the door marked forty-six, I heard Nana's familiar shuffle to the door.

As soon as she flung it open, I took her in. She was a tiny spitfire, with fluffy white curls, a bright green flowered dress, and her ever present dark blue slippers.

She hugged me harder than usual, almost squeezing me to bits. I wanted to fall to pieces and let the tears fall, but I forced myself to hold it together. "Eden, honey, how are you?"

"I'm good, thanks, Nana. How are you?"

She rolled her eyes behind her silver-framed glasses. "I'm disappointed that your mother didn't take her time on those stairs. Penelope has always run around more than she should have," Nana chuckled.

"She's doing fine," I said. "She'll be back at Uncle Nick's within a few days. Unless she'd rather stay here since there are no stairs. He's going to find out and let everyone know."

Nana nodded. "That's good." Then she gave me the strangest sideways grin. "From broken legs to broken hearts. I think it's time we had a cup of tea."

Following her around the corner, I smiled at the huge

brass plate engraved with an old-fashioned sailboat that was on her wall. It was one of her beloved knick-knacks that she brought over from England years ago. I passed the family portraits, then turned to where I could smell the fresh pot of tea before I saw it. Stepping into the kitchen, everything was in its place as it always was.

Except that Eric was sitting at the table.

**24**

———

ERIC

** Tea Time **

I wasn't the sort of person who believed that things happened for a reason. But it was darn handy that I got hold of Eden's grandmother's address just before I really needed it. There was no way to know where Eden might be headed, but I needed to get there quickly, just in case.

Some tenants leaving the building let me into the lobby. I made a mental note to speak to the property management company about security in this building. As I strode to the elevator, I almost laughed at myself. Eden just broke up with me, but my only thoughts were to protect her and her family.

I knew that it wasn't her real feelings. I also knew that being this pushy and showing up where I wasn't welcome would not win me any points.

It didn't matter anymore. I was down to the wire. Manners be damned.

Knocking softly on the door, I realized I was far more

nervous than I'd ever been before. I was used to meeting important, powerful people all the time, and had to instantly win them over. But now I was meeting an incredibly important woman with no appointment.

The door opened, and I instantly smiled at the sweet, white-haired lady in front of me. "Hello," I said. "Victoria Palmer?"

"Yes." She didn't look surprised or suspicious, just analytical, somehow.

I held out my hand. "Eric Stone. I'm a friend of Eden's."

"Hello, nice to meet you," she said, shaking my hand more firmly than I would have expected. "Come in," she said immediately. "Would you like a cup of tea?"

"Thank you, that's very kind," I said.

"Is Eden here in Vancouver?"

"She is," I said, following the wave of her hand to sit at her kitchen table. "She might be on her way here, actually. But I was hoping to have a word with you first."

Victoria looked me up and down carefully. "Businessman. You're working in an office a lot now, but you used to do very physical things. Like bricklaying, or construction or something." She cocked her head. "Thirty-eight?"

I grinned. She was immediately likable. "Thirty-seven, actually."

She took a sideways look at my shoes, then pulled out a teapot, rinsing it with hot water before putting the bags inside. "Your shoes are spotless. You're hoping to make a good impression. What did you want to talk about?"

Suddenly I didn't know where to start. I stared into space for a second, trying to collect my thoughts.

Victoria snapped her fingers in front of me. "Start from the middle. Start anywhere. Just spit it out."

I chuckled. "I can see why Eden takes your wisdom seriously."

She shrugged, pouring boiling water into the pot. "Eden is a sweet young lady, but she hasn't been around the block many times yet. She should still be listening to her elders." Her eyes flipped to me. "Her elder women, anyway."

"I completely agree. I've been gently encouraging Eden to listen to herself more. To her own guts. She's very timid in a lot of ways, and I'm hoping that she learns to trust her real feelings."

Victoria set out three teacups, placing the pot in the center of the table. "I like what you just said. Partly because I completely agree, but mostly because you're not firing me a line of horsefeathers that you think I want to hear."

I nodded. "I only want what's best for Eden. I feel that I could be an excellent partner for her. It's one of those feelings that strikes you straight down to the bones."

Victoria sat back with a delighted smile, nodding.

"Eden has a lot of fears, and a lot of things make her a bit nervous," I said carefully. "I don't want to tell her that she's wrong, or make light of her feelings because I don't agree with them. But I know that we belong together. It just might take her a bit of time to see that."

Victoria looked me dead in the eye. Then she leaned forward, unblinking, staring at me. I held still, unflinching. If she did have some mystical power and could see into people's souls, I had nothing to hide.

"You're straight up," she said, nodding. "You're also completely in love with her."

Trying to hold back the laughter, I said, "Yes, but I haven't told her that, so maybe that could be our little secret for now."

She reached out to pat my hand. "Don't keep things bottled up for too long," she said quite seriously.

"I agree, but considering that she broke up with me about half an hour ago, it's probably not appropriate today."

Her eyebrow raised. Her lips pursed. "What did you do?" she asked sternly, but her eyes were sparkling.

Trying to figure out how to begin to explain it, I was saved by a knock at the door.

# 25

## EDEN

** Gambling **

I couldn't believe Eric was sitting at my grandmother's kitchen table. It was impossible.

My body wanted to jump into his arms. To be comforted. To feel safe and warm, like I had somebody on my team that was going to help me get through this.

My mind screamed in terror, thinking that maybe his stalking tendencies were real. His devotion was sort of romantic on one level, but his lack of boundaries was questionable. I knew that he meant me no harm, but it was disconcerting. How did he even have this address?

My guts were the most decisive. I was livid.

"What in the sassafras are you doing here?" I hissed.

Nana put a hand on my shoulder. "Eden, Eric came here to ask for my advice. Apparently, you just dumped him, but he's not sure that's the most logical thing right now."

"We are not dealing with logic," I said slowly, glaring at Eric as sharply as I could. "There are greater forces at work here. He doesn't seem to understand how serious they are."

Eric stood up, and it felt like he took up the entire room. Remembering the gigantic chiseled physique that was hiding under his shirt and jacket was an unwelcome reminder of how much my body craved his.

"Eden, why don't we step into the hall for just a moment, so that you could tell me off without upsetting your grandmother?"

Nana laughed, sitting down and pouring herself a cup of tea while we went outside.

"How dare you," I muttered the second the door was shut behind us. "I just finished telling you that we can't be together for your own safety, and you just show up? Don't you have a self-preservation instinct?"

"I know that I am perfectly safe," he said.

"Well, how about the terror I'm feeling knowing that one of us could get hurt?"

He held out his hand, and I took it automatically. Instantly I felt that connection between us. That enchanting feeling of calm, mixed with simmering lust, and a deep need to be closer to him.

"You can't stalk me," I practically whimpered. "You know it's wrong."

"It's not stalking. It's a conversation in a safe place with your lovely grandmother right here for you." He paused. "Eden, I know you're scared of us being real. I can feel it. But you know that we're right together. We're so right, that you're going to forgive me for being a little bit wrong occasionally."

"What in the blazes does that even mean?"

He cocked his head, and those full lips turned up in a beautiful smile. "When there is a project I want, I go through every aspect of the deal carefully, eliminating any possibility of failure. I don't gamble. Not ever. I buy a lottery ticket a few times a year, just for fun, but when it comes to something important, I don't gamble at all."

"Are you saying that I'm a gamble?" I asked. I wasn't understanding him.

"No. I'm telling you that I'm going to gamble for the first time in my life. If you agree to be open-minded, what do you think of walking in and asking your grandmother whether we should stay together?"

I was so surprised that I actually took a step backward.

"No, wait," he said quickly, "I mean, date for as long as you'll have me. I don't mean that her word will be law, or that if I were to turn into a raving asshole ten years from now, you should stick with me. I just mean giving us a fair chance."

"You want to walk in there and ask her to decide for us?"

"Yes," he said. "Fifty-fifty odds. A coin flip. Based solely on your grandmother's opinion of me from us having spoken for about five minutes before you arrived."

"And if she says no?" I asked.

"Then we finish our tea and move on. I will still fly you home any way you like, and take care of your mother. But I will never contact you beyond an occasional text to politely inquire if you are well."

I took another involuntary step back, my shoulders thumping against the wall behind me.

I hated this idea. It was too much pressure. It was too cut and dried. It felt sort of creepy to leave the decision to someone else.

On the other hand, I loved this idea. If Nana said we should be together, that would be going against her own whispers. That would mean that we were meant to be, and we were probably safe.

Unless we weren't safe, and her contradicting herself got us both injured or killed.

Forcing myself to slow my breathing, I attempted to be logical. For the moment, we could let Nana decide. If she thought we should be together, then we could revisit everything tomorrow. Maybe I could ask Mom and Eva about the whispers again, and try to figure out how accurate they really were.

Feeling like my head was spinning, I mumbled, "Okay. Let's ask her."

We went in and sat at the table, while I tried to look as relaxed as possible. Nana poured us some tea, and the fragrance of her strange blend was instantly calming.

"Thank you," Eric said, taking a sip. "Wow, this is amazing."

Nana smiled. "It's always about creating balance by blending different things together." She flashed me a pointed look. "So, what's up with you two?"

I didn't know where to start, but thankfully Eric jumped in.

"We have a very important question for you," he said. "It might sound odd. Please know that we are absolutely serious, and genuinely interested in listening to every detail of what you have to say."

"All right," Nana said. "Go ahead."

"When you state prophecies for people, how often do they come true?"

I gasped, almost dropping my teacup. Setting it on the table, it rattled against the wooden surface as my hand shook.

"Prophecies?" Nana looked at me, but I had no idea what to say. "Why would you think I would ever have prophecies?" she asked with a bright chuckle.

"Apparently the members of your family have noticed that you sometimes zone out a bit, and mutter things to the ceiling. They take note of this, and those things sometimes come true."

Nana looked at him like he was completely off his rocker.

"You don't know about this at all?" Eric asked earnestly. "They call it The Knowing."

Nana's shoulders shook, then she absolutely cracked up laughing, setting down her teacup to push herself away from the table slightly. We had to wait a moment for her to catch her breath.

"Cheese and crackers, the things you kids think." She turned to look at me. "You think the things I randomly mutter are some sort of blessing or curse or whatever? Some sort of ancient truth telling? Honey, I'm not that old."

I realized that I was scarcely breathing, and starting to get dizzy. Forcing myself to take a few breaths, I finally said, "You told Eva never to drive in the freezing rain. Then when she did, she had an accident."

"Of course she did. Freezing rain is really dangerous. You know I watch the weather channel all the time."

"Okay. What about telling Mom that she should tell people when she's hurt? She didn't listen to that, and then she really got hurt when she fell down the stairs."

Nana looked completely perplexed. Then suddenly her eyes grew wide. "Bloody hell. Do you mean when I look up and whisper song lyrics to myself?"

I blinked hard. "What?"

Eric looked like he was trying not to explode with laughter.

Nana laughed brightly, getting up to arrange a plate of sugar cookies. "Eden, it's one of my little tricks to stay right in the head as I'm getting older. I'm not old enough to be a crazy soothsayer yet. But if I get there, I want to still have my marbles."

She placed a tray of cookies in front of us and sat back down. "Sometimes when I remember a song lyric or a quote from a movie, I say it out loud so I'll remember to look it up later. It's a memory trick I read about. Something about looking up and to the left, and speaking the words aloud locks it in your memory better."

"So when you told Eden not to get into bed with the devil," Eric said softly, "That didn't mean anything?"

She shook her head. "That's an old country song. Fiddle-sticks, I did forget to look that one up."

Nana turned to me, grabbing my hand and squeezing it. "Eden, you look like you've seen a ghost. You know those things aren't real. None of that superstitious curses and hokum and whatnot is real. I thought you had a better head about you, girl."

My mind was spinning, and I actually felt a bit dizzy. Instead of screaming, I slowly ate a sugar cookie.

Eric helped himself to a cookie as well, then flashed me a smile. "So, Mrs. Palmer–"

"Victoria, please."

"Thank you. Victoria, since my original name had slightly devilish undertones, Eden was worried that us being together might bring bad luck and destruction upon us. I desperately want to give her my heart, but I don't want to keep running after her if that's not what she truly desires."

Looking up into his warm, deep eyes that were completely fixed on me, I was completely positive about which answer I wanted my grandmother to choose.

"I told Eden that instead of flipping a coin, we should let you decide. She obviously respects your opinion. You certainly don't know me very well, but based on the evidence in front of you, and your gut feeling, do you think that Eden and I should date?"

Nana's hand flew up to her necklace, touching the small diamonds that my grandfather had given her for their tenth anniversary. She always did that when she was overcome and needed a moment.

She turned to me. "Honey, there are a lot of lazy, careless, heartless men in this world. This one here," she said, nodding to Eric as if he couldn't hear her, "Came here to beg for my approval. I can't think of any reason why you shouldn't give him a fair shot."

"Thank you," I whispered to Nana, just before my throat closed completely.

Eric reached around the teapot to grasp my other hand. "It's okay. We're going to be alright."

As always, Nana knew how to lighten the mood. "Now, shall we talk about your clumsy mother? I have told that woman to slow the heck down when she gets running around. The woman never listens."

We finished our tea and cookies, and listened to several of Nana's gossipy stories about some of the other seniors in this complex who were, "Getting horizontal, if you know what I mean." Then it was time for us to leave.

Watching my grandmother hug the daylights out of Eric almost made my heart explode. It was at that moment that I realized I felt complete again.

As she hugged me, she whispered in my ear, "Your boyfriend is fucking hot. Get a piece of that."

"Nana!" I shrieked.

She giggled girlishly. "Whispers don't count as cursin'," she said with a wink.

**26**

———————

ERIC

** Quiet Dinner **

Eden was quiet as we walked to the elevator. It wasn't every day that a person found out that something their entire family believed was completely untrue. Leading her out of the building, I kept my hand on her lower back, but wanted to give her a bit of space.

"Are you all right?" I asked softly.

She nodded. It didn't seem like she could speak.

"Would you like me to take you to your Uncle's house, or get another room in my hotel for you?"

Eden looked up at me, her warm brown eyes so pretty in the light of sunset. "I'd like to stay with you."

"Okay. You seem spacey, so should I be pushy and take you back to the hotel? We can order in dinner, have a glass of wine, and chill out?"

"Perfect," she said, nodding.

Grabbing us a taxi, we got to the hotel quickly. As I checked us in, Eden was glued to my side. We weren't quite touching, she was just hovering. I hurried us up to the penthouse suite, where our luggage was already waiting.

"How did..." Eden blinked. "I was in such a rush to get to the hospital I forgot all about our luggage."

"My assistant told the plane service where we'd be staying, and they shipped it."

I walked her to the couch and sat Eden down, slipping her shoes off. "You're probably starving," I said. "What would you like for dinner?"

"I... I have no idea," she said.

"How about something simple? Burger and fries, or pasta? Maybe chicken fingers?"

Finally her eyes lit up. "Chicken fingers and onion rings, please."

Lifting her hand, I kissed the back of it, then went over to the desk phone to order. I came back to sit beside her, not sure what to do. Thankfully she snuggled against my shoulder, taking my hand.

"You must think I'm an idiot," she said sadly.

"Not in the slightest," I said emphatically. "Not the tiniest bit. People believe what their families believe. You believed what the evidence in front of you stated, and what your mother told you, even if that turned out not to be true."

Eden looked up to me with a hopeful smile. "So, I take it that you were hoping Nana would say we should be together?"

"Absolutely," I said. "I adore you. I hope it's obvious by now. I need us to be together. I know we are going to be ridiculously happy."

She nodded, opening her mouth to speak, but there was a sharp knock at the door. I ran to get our food, setting it out on the coffee table while the server quickly poured the wine and left.

I found an old comedy special on TV, and put that on quietly while we ate. Eden still seemed spaced out, but after she had some food, and a half glass of wine, she started laughing at the show more naturally.

As I started to clear away the plates, she gripped my wrist. "Thank you," she whispered.

"You're welcome," I smiled. "Was your dinner good?"

"Yes, it was better than I expected. But that's not what I mean." Her bottom lip trembled slightly, and I saw her breath hitch. "Thank you for not giving up on us."

Ignoring the dishes, I sat back and scooped her into my lap, holding her tightly. Pressing my lips to her ear, I breathed, "I will never give up on you, baby. Never. Even if we have a little fight here and there, I will never give up on you. I'll always put you first. You're my girl. I knew it from the second you smiled at me."

Her nose crinkled as she laughed. "Was it a deep, psychic feeling?"

"You can call it whatever you want. It wasn't The Knowing, I just knew it."

Her fingers wound into the back of my hair, pulling my lips to hers. The entire world melted away as we kissed softly, slowly, for what seemed like a very long time. Her body moved slightly against me, but this wasn't sexual. This was the two of us bonding. This was a deep feeling that we were both completely aware of, but hadn't really said yet.

"I should tell you something," I said as I finally pulled away so that we could breathe.

"What's that?"

"Since I've already told your grandmother, it would only be right to tell you as well." Her eyes were so pretty as she stared at me, waiting.

"Eden, I love you."

Her eyes fell closed for half a second, as a shiver ran through her. Then her eyelashes fluttered as she looked up at me coyly. "I love you, too. You know it's too soon to say this, though. I've known you for a week and a half."

"Absolutely. But I never want to keep secrets from you. So there it is."

She kissed me again, then her curvy body started moving against mine in a way that made it very clear what she was after.

"Wait," I said gently.

She stopped moving, and pouted, forcing me to nibble her bottom lip until she giggled.

"Someday when we have kids, we're going to have to keep a secret from them."

Eden rolled her eyes. "You don't want to tell them how Mommy nearly messed everything up because of some misheard song lyrics?"

"No," I laughed. "We're going to have to make up a more romantic story of how we met. There's no way we can tell them you bumped into me on a dance floor in a cheesy club. That's tacky."

Her laughter rang through the room, making me laugh again, both of us shaking against each other.

**27**

---

EDEN

** Bed with the Devil **

I was almost disappointed when Eric picked me up and set me beside him, but it gave me a chance to look around the room for the first time. I had been in such a fog when we arrived that I hadn't noticed how gorgeous the penthouse suite was. It was bigger than my whole apartment. The paintings alone looked like they belonged in a museum.

Eric noticed my wide eyed staring as he shuffled the dishes away. "One of the perks of starting your own company and having things go well," he said. "To be honest, I normally get a regular room, but I thought you might appreciate the extra space."

What I truly appreciated was the giant bed at the far end of the room.

"Do you want a bath, or shall we just go to bed?" Eric asked. "It's been a long day, and it's getting late, Toronto time."

"Bed," I nodded, digging in my suitcase for my toothbrush and some pajamas. When I came out in my little pink shorts and camisole, Eric was already in bed, looking like he had freshened up in the guest bathroom.

The lights were dim. The focus of the lovely, elegant room was the huge bed, where a shirtless hunk who loved me waited.

My happiness won over my exhaustion. Slipping in beside him, I curled against his massive shoulder, quickly realizing that he was naked.

"I prefer sleeping in the buff, but don't think I'm trying to send you any signals." He raised one eyebrow. "Unless you want me to send signals. But I completely understand if you just want to sleep. It's been a hell of a day. "

His hand skimmed down my spine, somehow hitting nerves I didn't even know I had.

"Do you know how I'm a bit nervous about practically everything?" I said softly.

"Yes. I'm going to do everything in my power to protect you and make things easier for you."

"Actually, I think I like it that you push me a bit. But also..." I had to pause and take a breath. "I'm trying very hard not to be scared of how intense we are together."

His hand passed down my back, then around the curve and up over my hip. I adored the way his fingers tightened on my skin, giving me a little shake.

"We can be gentle, or intense, or whatever you desire," he said softly. "As long as I know that we're together, I won't freak out and do crazy things anymore."

"Helping me speak up more means that I'm also going to be able to call you on your bull crap," I grinned.

"Absolutely, baby. I want you to keep me on my toes. I need you to tell me if I'm ever being an ass. Or if there's anything you need that I'm not giving you."

My exhaustion had already turned to an adrenaline rush, as my hand massaged his wide, firm chest. Part of me still couldn't believe that a man this breathtakingly hot seemed so obsessed with me. But a larger part of me knew that I should stop thinking stupid questions and show my man how I felt.

My hand slipped lower and gripped his thick, rock hard cock. I loved that I aroused him. I needed to give him everything. My hand moved up and down his shaft, my thumb swirling around the sensitive head while he exhaled was a long, low sigh.

"Is this your way of saying that you need to go to sleep immediately?" he grinned.

"No," I said, reaching down to pull off my shorts. "I'm giving you a very different message."

He ripped off my camisole, throwing me onto my back almost roughly. His lips met mine softly, but his wandering fingers were much more demanding. My thighs twitched with yearning as his fingertips spread me open, tickling along my labia until he parted my pussy lips and plunged a finger inside.

"Mmm, yes," I moaned into his mouth.

I loved it when he fisted my hair and controlled how hard I kissed him back. I loved the way he thrust inside me with his fingers. He didn't just slide mechanically in and out. Somehow his fingers twisted and turned, touching every nerve ending, and finding a little place near the front of my tunnel that made my hips twitch.

"That's the spot," he murmured. His thumb began circling my clit gently as he plunged a second finger inside. The pressure was wild, as he worked my body as if I were his toy.

His tongue dragged against mine greedily, as if he were

desperate to taste me. Reaching down to stroke him, I was clumsy and unfocused, already about to come.

Eric pulled back for air. I could almost feel his eyes raking over my skin as he watched my breasts heaving while I gasped.

"You are so fucking beautiful," he muttered, leaning in to suck on my nipple while I began to quiver. He stared into my eyes. "Come for me, Eden. Show me that you're mine."

I didn't know whether it was his pushy possessiveness, his insanely gorgeous body, or the earnest, sweet look in his eyes. Grabbing his bicep with one hand and his cock with the other, I shook from head to toe as the waves of my climax rumbled through me.

"Eric," I choked. The final shudder that ran through me was almost violent, and my eyes snapped open, locked on his.

I felt like I was in a trance. It was wild how easily he was able to draw me out of myself. He kissed me softly, as if I were the most precious thing in the world.

His lips skimmed along my cheekbone, murmuring, "I love hearing you say my name, but when you scream it like that, it fills me with very filthy urges."

Gripping his face in both hands, I nodded frantically. "Yes," I blurted. "Now."

Eric moved over me, spreading my legs wider and grazing the head of his shaft along my wet pussy lips. "You and I are going to be the best kind of trouble together," he grinned.

My pussy was flooded with juices. I felt swamped in heat. Need. My sensitive nipples brushed against Eric's hard chest as his weight began to bear down, sinking his cock inside me slowly. He took his time, pressing inside me carefully, deliberately. It felt even more like we were bonding.

"I love you so much, Eden," he whispered against my lips as he held perfectly still inside me.

"I love you, Eric," I breathed. "I want to kiss you every day and every night forever."

I realized I was being overly sappy, but he grinned, starting to move slowly in a deep, sensual rhythm. "Absolutely, baby."

His hand began massaging my breast, squeezing my nipple between his thumb and forefinger until I moaned.

"I've never been addicted to anything stronger than coffee, Eden. But I think you're going to be my favorite new addiction."

I nodded, my head falling back as the pace of his thrusts increased perfectly. Tangling my fingers in the back of his hair, I brought his lips to mine for a filthy, gritty kiss. I wanted him to feel my heat. I wanted him to feel how much I was overcome.

His husky groan rattled through both of us. He kissed me so hard my breathing faltered, and my gasping cries filled the room.

I could feel his thighs clenching, his hips rocking as he thrust deeply, lustily, again and again. "You're so tight, baby. I can't believe how good you feel. You're making me lose my mind."

"Good," I said with more sass than I expected.

I spread wider, wrapping my legs around his hips so he could plunge right to the end of my tunnel. The pressure was incredible. The blinding need for release twitched through me, just a hair out of reach.

Then his thumb found my clit, rolling over it gently as he pounded faster. "Tell me what I need to hear," he begged.

Looking up into those deep, gorgeous eyes, I was flooded with something beyond love. It just felt like... knowing.

Knowing that Eric was under my spell as much as I was under his. Knowing that such a huge, powerful man was also under my control. We needed each other, and our balance was going to fulfill us both.

"I love the way you fuck me," I whispered. "Is that what you want to hear, Eric? Do you want to hear how good your huge cock feels in my wet little pussy?"

His eyes were blazing as he increased his speed even more. "Fuck, don't stop," he barked.

"Fuck me deeper with that luscious cock," I moaned. Then I squealed as the heat rushed through me like a brushfire. My stomach clenched, my toes and fingers curled. I twitched helplessly under him while he smiled, watching with absolute adoration.

As soon as I blinked and caught my breath, the world tilted. I was on all fours, Eric's arm under my stomach as he drove into me with a passion that was startling.

"You said you wanted it deeper, baby," he said, biting along the back of my shoulder blade.

His hand reached around for my clit again. He was ramming me, shaking me so hard. It only took a few tiny strokes across my swollen, oversensitive nub before I screamed again, fisting the sheets as my ass ground back against him.

"Oh fuck," I shrieked, "Come inside me. Please..."

His savage growl unhinged me. His heat flooded me. He shook against me hard from the force of his climax. As he finally came to a stop, I turned back over my shoulder to kiss him. Then he leaned back with his hands on my hips, looking completely dazed.

He gently withdrew, collapsing on the bed beside me, entwining his fingers with mine as I laid on my side.

"Holy squid," I finally murmured.

"Indeed," he said, nodding.

After a couple of minutes, he pulled me into his arms, kissing me, then rocking me against his chest. "Can't make words," he muttered. "Love you. Sleep."

I pulled the blanket over us, and as he nodded off, I felt completely, utterly bonded to this man.

He was mine. Forever. I just knew.

## 28

### ERIC

*Morning Business Meeting*

I t was incredibly hard to sleep. A decision popped into my head when I first tried to close my eyes. Throughout the whole night, I barely managed to doze off a few times. As the sun began to stream in the windows, I practically held my breath until Eden's eyes fluttered open.

"Hi," she murmured.

"Good morning." I sat up. "Business meeting."

Eden laughed, rolling toward me. "Before coffee? Isn't that like... Er, what's the term for not being able to make legal decisions because you're not in your right mind?"

Damn. Even when she was barely awake, she always made me laugh. "Mental incompetence. But I'm sure you're fine."

Giving her a gentle kiss, I murmured, "What was that non-curse thing you say... sweet fancy dancers?"

She giggled. "Yeah."

"Sweet fancy dancers, you're pretty."

Making her blush was going to be one of my favorite daily activities. Kissing her again, she started to move toward me, but I leaned away. "Business meeting."

I grabbed my phone, calling up some photos I'd found in the middle of the night. "We're negotiating a deal here. The terms will have a visual reminder on your finger. This morning we're going to a specialty jewelry store and getting you a statement ring."

"Huh? What sort of statement?"

I showed her a couple of massive diamond rings, loving the way her wide brown eyes sparkled in confusion.

"Well, I would like to make one of three declarations with it. You can choose which one. Then we'll go shopping and you can choose the ring you like best to remind us daily of the statement."

She sat up straight, tucking the sheet around her, unfortunately covering her luscious boobs. "I'm listening."

"Statement one. I'm wildly in love with you and we're together. The ring shall be worn as a token of my love and devotion."

Her eyes softened. "I like that."

"Statement two. I'm wildly in love with you and we're together. We shall be married in a reasonable time frame of your choosing. The ring shall be worn as a token of our engagement, and a band will be added at our wedding, whenever that turns out to be."

Eden's eyes looked hazy. She blinked hard. "Are you..."

"I will when I have the ring in my hand, yes."

"Oh." She stared at me, then down at her hands. Then she smiled. "You said there was an option three?"

"Yes. It's the same as statement two, but we get married tonight, while we're here with your Nana."

"Oh." Her hands were shaking and she looked completely flustered.

"Shh," I pulled her into my arms. "Breathe, baby."

Eden nodded against my chest, and I was struck once again by how perfectly she fit against me.

"Are you a huge wedding girl? A tiny wedding girl, or anything in between?"

"I don't know." She looked baffled.

I began to laugh. "Damn. I'm sorry. I assumed that all women had their weddings planned out since they were seven."

"Not me." Eden took a deep breath, relaxing against me. She took another slow breath, thinking. "What if we took one year? We'll plan something small and simple, but have some time to think everything through."

I took her hands, holding them between us. "To hell with the ring part. Eden, will you marry me?"

Her face lit up as she grinned, nodding. "Yes."

I kissed her gently, leaning back so that she was on top of me. "You'll move into my place right away?"

She placed a hand on my chest. "Well, not right away."

She must have seen my face fall, but she shook her head. "I'm going to have to clean and organize everything," she said very seriously. "And I have another essay due next week. So it might take me at least two or three weeks."

Flipping her, I pinned her hands over her head, kissing along her throat. "I'm going to do everything in my power to be the best fiancé ever."

"I know you're going to be an amazing husband," she murmured.

"Yeah?" I kissed her nose. "How do you know that? Do you have magic knowing powers?"

She struggled to free her wrists and I released her so that she could wrap her hands around my shoulders. "You listen to me. You care for me. You're always building me up, and have never once torn me down. I can't wait to be your wife, but after how fast all of this has been, we shouldn't rush."

"You're going to hear this a lot over the next sixty-something years," I chuckled. Then I made my voice sound nasal as I sing-songed, "Yes, dear. Anything you say."

Her bright laugh filled the room more than the sunlight streaming in the windows. "I love you," she giggled.

"I love you, little miss paradise."

** What's in a Name, Again **

*** Almost Two Years Later ***

"Mary?"

"Too plain."

"Edna?"

"Too old fashioned." I could hear my breath becoming raspy.

"Marsha? Mmm..." Eric's tongue circled my clit again. Son of a pirate... he was getting so good at knowing exactly what I needed. "Damn, you are delicious."

"Please," I choked. "Could you focus on one thing at a time?"

His thick fingers slid out of my twitching, drenched pussy. "I'm not letting you come until you decide on a name."

His other hand reached up to caress my rounded stomach. Feeling my body stretch and change with our daughter had left me wildly aroused from the second I got pregnant.

Which was carefully arranged not to happen until after we'd been married for several months. Eric was weirdly old fashioned about that, which I found charming.

He'd been teasing me for nearly half an hour now, which I found less than charming.

"Please," I gasped, "I'll let you name her whatever you want if you make me come right now."

I knew he wouldn't hold me to it, and we had another month and a half to decide. But right now I was about to explode.

His tongue flattened against my clit, swirling slow and steady as his fingers thrust deep. I could feel the heat building in my hips, as my hands clutched his shoulders. Those dark, deep eyes stared at me, and I was unable to control myself.

"Fuck... oh, fuck, harder," I whispered. His eyes grinned up at me as he dug in, adding a third finger and grinding his tongue against me.

"Jesus fucking fuck..." I squealed, the rush of tingling heat washing through me as I rode his mouth into oblivion.

Collapsing back onto our giant bed, I blinked up at the ceiling, then addressed it as he would. "Well, now. Should I let my gorgeous husband take me, or should I have him make me dinner first?"

Before I could stop laughing, Eric had turned me onto my side, spooning me as he lifted my top leg. My moaning filled our bedroom as he stroked the head of his shaft along my dripping pussy lips, then I squealed as he plunged slowly inside.

The pressure of his thick length thrilled me every single day. Often two or three times a day. I especially loved it lately when he took me from behind like this so that he could pound me hard without worrying about putting pressure on the baby.

Our sex was always surprising, and often not in our bed. But the past few weeks I'd really 'bloomed' as he put it, and this bump had come between us a tiny bit.

His fingers gripped my hips tightly, driving deep. Twisting over my shoulder, I kissed him hard, rough. Then his hand slid over my hip, reaching around to flicker his fingertips across my clit.

"Goddamn it," I nearly growled, "That feels amazing."

"I hope our daughter never hears us in bed," he murmured. I could hear the heat in his voice. The raspy tone whenever he was driving into me. "You're going to teach her all sorts of colorful language."

"Fuck me harder," I gasped.

"Yes, dear. Anything you say."

His hips rolled against me in a deep, perfect rhythm. Then Eric began thrusting up into me jerkily, roughly, the way he knew I loved it.

His bottom hand reached up to grip my much heavier breast, and I could sense how much he liked them bigger. His squeezing and groping sent sparks straight through me, as I reached around to grab his ass.

My entire body was starting to twitch as I panted with raw desire. Eric's teeth sunk into my shoulder, the tiny nip of pain adding to my pleasure, making me scream.

"Yeah, baby, let me hear it. Let me hear you when you come all around me."

"Yes..." I choked.

I loved it when he was a bit rough, a bit savage. As much as I adored it when he made love to me, there was something extra in the way he fucked me.

The pressure of his thickness against my inner walls

increased, and I could feel how close he was. "Oh fuck," he muttered, "You feel so perfect, baby."

"Fuck almighty," I screamed, not caring if the windows were open. Every muscle tightened as I came, twitching and squealing, my pussy fisting Eric's cock so hard I'm surprised it didn't hurt him.

"Yes, gorgeous," he breathed. "Oh, Eden..." I felt his heat flood me, screaming again with another mini-climax from the sensation of his release.

We rocked together as our bodies took complete control, then finally found our breath. Rolling to face him, I cupped his face in my hand. "I love you so much."

He kissed my nose, then grinned wickedly. "I love you, baby. Even though that's the last time I'll be taking you that hard for a while, you know I love you."

My bottom lip thrust out in a pout, and he caught it in his teeth. "You're outrageously sexy," he mumbled.

"Nope, that's you," I laughed. "But you're never, ever to tease me for that long again. If you don't let me come, next time I'll strangle you with my thighs."

His dark eyes blazed. "I get to choose the name. You promised."

My eyes narrowed as I glared. "We'll keep chatting." I couldn't stifle my giggle.

Eric sat up, pulling me with him. "But I have the perfect name."

"Okay. Hit me."

His crazily handsome grin nearly distracted me as he paused for dramatic effect. Finally he said, "Tori."

I blinked hard, tears instantly brewing. Tori. For my grandmother, Victoria.

As I burst into happy sobs, Eric rolled his eyes. "Dammit. I should have known after you cried at that phone commercial last night." Pulling me into his arms, he rocked me gently.

"It's perfect," I sniffled. "Thank you."

"Even if it didn't have such a lovely meaning for us, it's a cute name. It's perky. Then she could grow into the longer version later if she wants to."

Snuggling against Eric's shoulder, I could almost picture her. Our little Tori in pigtails, prancing around the backyard, making up games with Eric and I in the summer sun. Someday, our daughter Victoria, going to university, and becoming... anything she wants.

"Hey, dreamy girl," Eric murmured. "Where did you go?"

I smiled up at him. "Excited about the future."

"Do you want a prophecy to tell you how it's going to turn out?"

I shook my head. "No. Never. Let's just watch how everything unfolds."

He kissed me gently, in that magical way of his where there was no future and no past. Time stopped until we were breathless.

# ALSO BY HALEY TRAVIS

### Her New Bodyguard: Jackson

Ashley was so sexy and innocent that my need to care for her was far more than professional.

### Never Date The Boss

Ashley was talked into one little "business date" with her boss, and everything changed in a heartbeat. Or rather, a flutter of them.

### Never Kiss The Boss

One little drink. One little party night with the girls. One huge mystery man and a heart-flipping makeout session. Then one giant, sexy problem...

### Mackton Mechanics

Rev your engines and get ready to fall for these hot mechanics! These huge, rough men are comfortable working with steel. What will happen when they're tinkering with a sweet girl's heart instead of a motor?

### Daddy's Billionaire Boss

When Emily discovers her Dad's boss is the improbable man her aunt predicted she'd fall for, can she fit into his world?

### Daddy's Billionaire Doctor

When Lydia discovers her Dad's doctor is slightly obsessed with her, can she listen to her heart and take a chance?

### Daddy's Billionaire Best Friend

When Nora and her Dad's best friend end up in a hotel room together, the start of her summer was suddenly a lot more exciting!

## Mr. Right... As Rain

A gorgeous man saved me on the way to an interview. Maybe it was the good luck kiss from a stranger, but isn't falling in love so fast just a fantasy?

## Teased by my Roommate

A new roommate named Hawk. He's breathtaking, sexy, and I've already seen FAR too much of him. Now he'll never stop teasing me. But I love it.

## Diablo: Dirty Sinners

*Can this devil atone for his many sins?*

A filthy rich man with an even filthier reputation had no right to even touch an angel like Avery. But if she needed protection, she would get everything I had.

## Fake Summer Boyfriend

I'm terrified of giant men. But when Leif volunteered to scare off my stalker by pretending to be my boyfriend, I knew the gorgeous hulking security tech was the perfect man for the job.

## The Last Date

I was infatuated with Sasha. I will tease her, even court her, until I make her mine. Forever.

Please join the mailing list at

www.haleytravisromance.com

for new releases, updates, discounts & freebies!